THE I

SERIES TITLES

The Commission of Inquiry
Patrick Nevins

Maximum Speed
Kevin Clouther

Reach Her in This Light
Jane Curtis

The Spirit in My Shoes
John Michael Cummings

The Effects of Urban Renewal on Mid-Century America and Other Crime Stories
Jeff Esterholm

What Makes You Think You're Supposed to Feel Better
Jody Hobbs Hesler

Fugitive Daydreams
Leah McCormack

Hoist House: A Novella & Stories
Jenny Robertson

Finding the Bones: Stories & A Novella
Nikki Kallio

Self-Defense
Corey Mertes

Where Are Your People From?
James B. De Monte

Sometimes Creek
Steve Fox

PRAISE FOR

CLOSE CALL

"Whether it's death or regret, a laugh or a snicker, healing or ignoring what's coming; love, life, oh you know, *what people do*, Kim Suhr sucks you right in, comfy as can be, until *you didn't see it coming* opens a window on human nature, and there is a piercing little poke right in your heart."

—SANDRA SCOFIELD
National Book Award finalist
author of *Little Ships*

"The clarity, humor, and inventiveness of Kim Suhr's work is a joy. I'm so grateful for Suhr's voice and her beautiful, sharp sensibility."

—JANE HAMILTON
author of *The Excellent Lombards*

"*Close Call* gets us close—we slip in and out of various bodies just in time to start squirming. Over and over we stand at the precipice, in that suspended moment between what's happened and what still might, contemplating what-ifs. Adults imagine the best versions of themselves while knowing they're falling short. Children witness circumstances before they have the benefit of context—like why that traveling salesman makes Mom act so differently, or when innocently playing school takes a chilling turn. In this eclectic collection that plays with form and style, there's not a single wasted page."

—MAGGIE GINSBERG
author of *Still True*

"Kim Suhr is a natural storyteller, and the dazzling variety of tales in *Close Call* is all the proof a reader needs. Whether realist stories illustrating the complicated lives of men and women trying to solve the problems of life and relationships, or experimental bursts of innovative forms, all of it is filled with playful humor, tightly crafted sentences, and devastating pathos."

—ROBERT LOPEZ
author of *Good People*

"In Kim Suhr's *Close Call*, readers will discover stories of finely wrought craft and beautifully developed characters. These stories also showcase an astonishing array of fresh and surprising forms: text message tales, interconnected scripts, eulogies, and the progression of communication from pay phones to cells. Through this unique and expressive range, her characters come alive in their authentic striving to survive their own flaws. These are generous stories with great heart and tenderness toward the human condition."

—ANNE-MARIE OOMEN
Michigan Author Award Winner
author of *The Long Fields*

"Kim Suhr's writerly curiosity floats like a fine, shimmering mist over the stories in *Close Call*: what if, what if, what if... Through deft experiments in form and other narrative devices, Suhr and her characters explore the possibilities that arise from faith, duty, love, magic, loneliness, and community. *Close Call* is a finely rendered collection of stories told in a sure and strong voice."

—PATRICIA ANN MCNAIR
author of *Temple of Air*

CLOSE
stories
CALL

Kim Suhr

For Eva,
I hope you
enjoy these
stories as
much as I
did writing
them!
Kindly,
Kim

CORNERSTONE PRESS
UNIVERSITY OF WISCONSIN-STEVENS POINT

Cornerstone Press, Stevens Point, Wisconsin 54481
Copyright © 2024 Kim Suhr
www.uwsp.edu/cornerstone

Printed in the United States of America by
Point Print and Design Studio, Stevens Point, Wisconsin

Library of Congress Control Number: 2024942450
ISBN: 978-1-960329-46-2

Cover design by Ellen Suhr.

This is a work of fiction. Names, characters, businesses, places, events, and incidents
are either the products of the author's imagination or used in a fictitious manner. Any
resemblance to actual persons, living or dead, or actual events is purely coincidental.

Cornerstone Press titles are produced in courses and internships offered by the
Department of English at the University of Wisconsin–Stevens Point.

DIRECTOR & PUBLISHER
Dr. Ross K. Tangedal

EXECUTIVE EDITORS
Jeff Snowbarger, Freesia McKee

EDITORIAL DIRECTOR
Ellie Atkinson

SENIOR EDITORS
Brett Hill, Grace Dahl

PRESS STAFF
Chloe Cieszynski, Sophie McPherson, Eva Nielsen, Ava Willett

For Rob
again and always

ALSO BY KIM SUHR:

Nothing to Lose

CONTENTS

SIGNS

THE DIP

ERADICATED

SIGNS

JEWEL TEA

Bo barked before the doorbell had a chance to ring. I could feel the excitement level of the whole house change. Mom stubbed out her cigarette, took one last swallow of Pepsi, and closed her paperback. I turned myself right-side up on the recliner and ran for the door, grateful for the distraction.

"Well, hi there, Little Miss, is your mom at home?"

I didn't appreciate the "little" comment but decided to cut the man on the other side of the screen door some slack, just for something to do. His blue shirt had dark armpit stains, and the plaid of his pants made me woozy. He held a black suitcase-type thing that looked like it was made of extra-thick cardboard. What could be in that case? What business did he have with my mother?

"Yes, I am," Mom's voice startled me. "Carol, grab the dog."

"Well, hello there." His eyes twinkled. A dimple appeared on his right cheek. He looked much nicer when he smiled. "I'm your Jewel Tea Man. May I come in and show you some of my samples?"

I expected Mom's usual dismissal, *We don't buy from solicitors.* In fact, I had already turned to walk away thinking the show was over when Mom, in a voice I'd never heard before, said, "Well, why not? Come on in."

The Jewel Tea Man looked as surprised as I felt. Our neighborhood was pretty tough on door-to-door salesmen. Mom was probably his first taker all day.

"Now, you just make yourself comfortable, Ma'am." He set down his case in front of the couch. "I'll show you what I've got."

Bo barked louder and struggled to escape my grasp. "Carol, put that dog in the basement."

By the time I returned, he'd flipped open a cardboard box with a display of spatulas and other cooking utensils. He explained their uses and value. Mom shook her head.

Undaunted, he moved on to the cleaning supplies, brownie and cake mixes, scented soaps and candles. Nope. Nope. Nope.

I started to feel sorry for Mr. Jewel Tea. Sweat beads coated his upper lip. A trickle of perspiration traced his hairline on the way to his jaw, but the smile never left his face.

"Now can I assume, Ma'am, that there's a Mr.—?" He left a blank.

"Simmons. Yes. There's a Mr. Simmons."

"Well, then, you might want to buy a little something with Mr. Simmons in mind. We have some wonderful perfume called *Misty Romance*. It's guaranteed to make him sit up and take notice, although how he could miss a fine woman like you is beyond me."

My mother's hand went first to her hair, then to her neck. It twisted her wedding ring. The *nopes* that had dripped so easily from her lips earlier seemed to dry up.

Mr. Jewel Tea capitalized on his opening. "Of course, if he's the jealous type, he wouldn't let you wear it out in public. He'd have to beat the other fellas off with a stick."

Mom considered this. "Jealousy isn't his strong suit. Maybe a little *Misty Romance* is just what we need around here."

He gave each of her wrists a squirt. She rubbed them together, put one to her nose and inhaled a long, deep breath.

I expected her to give the next whiff to me, but instead, she waved her wrist in front of Mr. Jewel Tea's nose.

I couldn't believe what I was watching. My mother talking to a perfect stranger about her love life with my dad, waving her perfumed wrist in front of his pinchy nostrils. Too grossed out for words, I made a big show of leaving the room but stayed close enough to the doorway to hear what came next.

"Well, I tell you what. If I can talk you into ordering a set of dishtowels, I'll throw in a bottle of the *Misty Romance* toilet water for free."

Silence. Then, "Kenny can hardly object if it's free, can he?"

Now she was plotting with the Jewel Tea Man to get something called toilet water for free. She filled out the order form and offered to write him a check.

"Oh, no, Ma'am. You pay on delivery. I'll be back in four weeks. Every first Thursday is my day in New Brighton. Are you sure I can't interest you in a set of wooden spoons?"

But the moment was over. My mom was closing back up into her one-tough-customer mode and dismissing Mr. Jewel Tea Man.

I WATCHED THE CALENDAR anticipating his return, curious to see how Mom would treat him when the weather was cooler and she knew he was coming.

On the morning he was supposed to return, she was up earlier than usual, applied not only her eyebrows but mascara and a touch of blush on each cheek, too. On his way out the door, my father took note. "You look different today, Joyce. Got an appointment?"

"No, nothing special," she lied. I knew as well as she did the *appointment* that awaited us both.

Mom busied herself dusting the living room, a task that kept her near the door, didn't require much effort, and could be dropped at the ring of a doorbell. Next, she set in alphabetizing her romance novels. When she moved on to the album collection, I announced that I was hungry and couldn't she please make me some macaroni and cheese?

"Oh, for pity's sake. Can't you do *any*thing yourself?" She left the pile of albums and headed for the kitchen.

I was sure this would make the doorbell ring—a watched pot and all that—but it didn't. Not while she organized Dad's pipes. Not while she ironed his shirts. When the bell hadn't rung by 4:30, we both gave up. Mom changed into her usual t-shirt and pedal pushers. I headed to my tire swing in the backyard.

NEXT DAY, MOM GOT MOTIVATED to wash the windows and insisted I help. We tied up Bo in the backyard and wrapped our heads in bandanas, slid our sweaty hands into rubber gloves. She had read an article about using vinegar and newspaper to avoid streaks, and we were going to give it a try. We'd started on the third set of windows when the doorbell rang.

Mom kept the soggy newspaper moving across the window while she leaned to look toward the screen door. "Get that. Will ya?"

"Jewel Tea Man!" A voice called through the screen door. "Anybody home?"

I stood between the living room and the entryway, able to see both of them before they saw each other. Mom took off her gloves but left the bandana on her head. She pulled a few strands of her hair from under it, so they rested stylishly on either side of her face. I hadn't noticed it earlier, but she was wearing mascara again and a touch of light blue eye shadow. She stubbed out the cigarette that waited in the ashtray, tucked in her t-shirt.

Jewel Tea Man was smoothing down his already smooth hair. With the comb lines, it looked like a wheat field at the end of summer.

"Oh, that's right. I let *you* talk me into buying something, didn't I?" Mom's voice had a girlish quality, which I didn't care for. At all.

"I caught *you* in the middle of something now, didn't *I*?" His inflection mirrored hers. "I won't be but a minute then." He held up a package in one hand, a small lavender box in the other. "Dishtowels," he smiled, "and *Misty Romance* toilet water for Mrs. Simmons."

"I'll get my checkbook." Mom headed for her purse. "Carol, hold the door open for the Jewel Tea Man."

He stepped through the door but left his case on the porch. I went to reach for it to help him in, hoping the distraction of his sales pitch could break up the monotony of the vinegar and newspaper for a while.

"You can leave that right there, Carol." My hand stopped at the sound of my name. "I won't interrupt your mom's hard work by doing my dog and pony show today."

"Nonsense." Mom was back with a pen poised to write the check. "You've gone to the trouble of delivering my items. The least I can do is see what you've got. How much do I owe you?"

"Here's the receipt." He handed Mom the package, pinching the receipt against the toilet water with his thumb. "And no, thank you anyway. I want to have you as my customer for a long time, Mrs. Simmons, and interrupting your work of the day would prevent that. I'll stop back again next month." He took the check Mom offered, folded it in half, tucked it into his shirt pocket and turned to go. "I do thank you for your business. See you next month!"

Mom called to him just before he got to the end of our walk, "I thought Thursday was your day in New Brighton."

He came back a few steps toward our house. "You were expecting me yesterday, weren't you?" His mouth turned up at the corners like he was doing a fake smile, but there was something kind in his eyes, a little like he felt sorry for Mom. "We had a meeting with the new district manager, set my whole schedule back a day. I'll be back the Friday after Labor Day. Then back to Thursdays after that. If it's okay to come back that is."

Mom's "of course" came out before he finished his sentence.

THE FRIDAY AFTER LABOR DAY was a half-day at school. I watched the clock all morning while Mrs. Stevens droned on and on. And on. When the bell finally rang, I took off like a shot, skipped my usual stop at the corner store for a Jolly Rancher, and cut through three alleys on my way home.

As I reached to open the screen door, my mom's sing-songy voice spilled from the living room. A deep voice chuckled in response. Mr. Jewel Tea was back.

I wasn't sure whether I wanted to eavesdrop on their conversation or announce my arrival, so I wouldn't see something I wished I hadn't. My heavy book bag made the decision for me when it slipped off my shoulder with a thud.

"Carol, are you all right?" Normally, Mom would have come out to check, but she stayed inside waiting for an answer.

"Yeah, I'm fine." I stepped inside.

"Hiya, Carol." Mr. Jewel Tea winked at me. "Your mom and I were just looking at," he looked around, picked up a pink bottle, "bubble bath." He held it out to me. "Doesn't that smell nice?" He twisted off the cap.

I thought about telling him that bubble bath can give you a bladder infection but knew this comment would not be welcome.

"Yes, Carol, what do you think? Shall we give this a try?"

We? Since when did Mom buy bubble bath and then share it with me? Since when did she use the word, *shall*?

I shrugged.

"Okay, then it's settled. Time to do your homework. Go on, now."

Maybe I could get a snack out of her. "Can I have a cookie first?"

"You can have two but eat them in the kitchen." She didn't wait to see if I needed anything else. "So, I'll take one bottle of the bubble bath and some of that aftershave for Kenny."

Mr. Jewel Tea would be back in October.

"JOYCE, WHAT'S THIS CHECK made out to Jewel Tea?" Dad was balancing the checkbook at the kitchen table. He didn't balance the checkbook every month like Ruth Walsh's dad did. My dad would pull it out when things at work were getting tense and he needed to let off steam. I think cursing at a checkbook kept him from taking it out on Mom and me.

"Oh, just for this and that, for the kitchen." She didn't tell him about the toilet water or the bubble bath or the aftershave due to arrive the following week.

"Well, I'll be damned." Instead of sounding perturbed, he sounded delighted. "Look here. When you entered the check amount in the register, you subtracted wrong. We've got $102.63 more in checking than we thought we had."

Mom's uncomfortable look turned to one of relief. "Well, that's just like found money, Kenny. We should celebrate!"

Their voices dropped. I turned back to the *Brady Bunch* knowing Dad was too practical than to have a celebration over "found money" he hadn't really lost, so I was more than surprised when Mom stood in the living room doorway, her purse hanging from her shoulder, a tissue between her lips blotting her lipstick. "Come on, Carol. We're going to *Arby's*."

Dad came down the stairs, his hair combed and wearing a button-down shirt.

"Don't you look snappy!" Mom planted a kiss on his cheek then lingered over rubbing the lipstick smudge with her thumb.

Dad looked surprised. He took a deep breath, obviously noticing her new fragrance. "I've gotta keep up with you now, don't I?"

IT GOT TO THE POINT WHERE I could tell when Mr. Jewel Tea was expected without even looking at the calendar. Since I was usually in school when he came, he never got a chance to flash me his, "Hiya, Carol" smile and wink, but there were always artifacts of his having been there. Fudge brownies coming out of the oven cradled in brand new hot mitts. My mom wearing a gingham apron as she placed the meatloaf on the table. The smell of Jewel Tea aftershave lingering in the air.

Mom's face always had a different look to it after Mr. Jewel Tea had been there. My dad never said anything directly, but he seemed to pick up on changes in Mom, too. Apparently, the meatloaf tasted a little better when it was served by someone wearing a gingham apron because Dad's compliments were heartier than usual.

"Joyce, this has to be the best meatloaf you've ever made. Gimme another piece."

"Finally as good as your mother's?"

He burped through closed lips. "Better." His hand rested on her butt as she spatulaed another piece onto his plate.

"Well, it tastes like barf to me." I don't know where the words had come from, and, the minute they left my lips, I knew they were a big mistake. I could almost taste the Ivory soap on my tongue. Instead, Dad looked at Mom and said with a wink, "I'll take her piece!"

"*I'll* give you an extra piece," Mom purred.

I didn't understand the chuckle they shared. What was funny about that?

ON THE DAY OF MR. JEWEL TEA's next delivery, I faked sick. I couldn't put a name to what I was afraid of, but I knew that another man in our house alone with my mother would amount to no good. Two summers ago, Ruth Walsh's mom had "taken up with" (Mom's words) Ruth's brother's hockey coach. Now Coach Miller was Ruth's stepfather, and Ruth only got to see her weekly-checkbook-balancing dad every other weekend.

I decided to fake a case of strep throat. Maybe that would keep me home from school where I could keep an eye on things.

Mom shook the mercury back down in the thermometer. "You don't have a fever."

"Well, my throat hurts, and I have a headache." I scrunched my face and feigned a painful swallow.

"Tell you what," she opened my closet door, "get dressed and have some breakfast. You'll feel better once you get moving."

Part of me wanted to do as she said. Go to school. Let her take up with Mr. Jewel Tea Man. Leave it to the adults. The other part of me wanted to crawl under the covers and stand guard over the life I knew.

"I can't go, Mom. I promise I'll stay in bed all day if I don't go to school. You'll never even know I'm here."

By now, I was used to her Jewel Tea appearance: makeup, hair done, shoes instead of slippers, but I wasn't prepared for what came next. She pulled a pair of jeans and a sweater from my dresser and dropped them on my bed. Case closed.

I could hardly see across the room through my tears. Sure, I wasn't really sick, but, if I were, what kind of mom treats her sick kid that way? My stomach lurched at the thought of Mr. Jewel Tea becoming my stepdad. I dressed, grabbed my bookbag, marched down the stairs, and slammed the door behind me.

The school day passed with little incident. Teachers asked about my homework but took pity on me when I said I didn't feel good. "You poor thing," Mrs. Stevens said when I told her that my mom had sent me to school not feeling well.

At lunchtime, I realized I had left my sack lunch on the counter at home where it was every morning—or at least where it had always been before Mr. Jewel Tea came along. For all I knew, Mom had gotten so sidetracked by her mascara application that she'd forgotten to pack me a lunch all together. Obviously, she hadn't noticed I forgot it. Normally, she'd drop it off for me and I'd get called down to the office to pick it up. Not today. With no money, I was left to mooch fries from Rosie and hope Mandy would share part of her jelly sandwich.

My stomach was still so flippy from the morning that nothing tasted very good anyway. I had to force down the brownie Rosie shared with me, the image of Mrs. Walsh holding hands with Coach Miller vivid in my mind.

Gym class was next. We all moaned when Mr. McHenry told us we'd be doing the mile run for the Presidential Fitness Challenge. My weak performance in the sit-up portion the week before had already knocked me out of the running for a certificate, but I'd have to run the mile anyway. About two-thirds of the way through, I rounded the basketball hoop, saw stars, and crumpled to the ground.

I came to, propped up in Mr. McHenry's arms, his voice loud in my ear. "… get the nurse. Carol, you okay?" And I was out again.

Next thing I knew, I was in the nurse's office, and before long Mom was standing over me with a look of concern I'd never seen before.

A male figure stood in the doorway, not in my dad's work blues, though. It was Mr. Jewel Tea in his woozy plaid pants.

"Dehydrated" and "no lunch" and then "ER" and "just to be sure" filtered through my fog. Soon, I was in the front seat of Mr. Jewel Tea's car, sandwiched between him and my mom.

"Sorry we can't fit you in the back seat there, Carol. I'm afraid we'd lose you among all those samples." He flicked his blinker. "We'll get you to the hospital in just a few minutes anyway."

"Why—?" I couldn't finish my question.

At the hospital, I choked down a bag of Fritos my mom bought from a vending machine and drank a Dixie cup of water. While I waited to be seen, Mr. Jewel Tea was mistaken for being my dad three different times. When they'd offer a form for a parent to sign, he'd show them his palms. "Just a friend of the family." He made a face at the clipboards like they had fungus on them. Mom's body tensed a little more with each refusal.

"This is ridiculous. I'm going to get things moving." She headed for the receptionist. Finally, a nurse took me back to an exam room for an IV to get some moisture back into my parched body.

LATER, WHEN WE PULLED UP TO OUR HOUSE, my dad's work truck was already in the driveway. If I wasn't already nauseated, this sight would have sent bile into my throat.

Dad stood on the porch looking like he expected the driver of this unfamiliar, rusty Pontiac to do a y-turn in the driveway and head back the opposite direction as so many others did when they realized they'd pulled onto a dead-end street.

Mom grabbed the door handle when she saw him. "Shit!"

I don't know what was more foreign, the word in my mother's mouth or the sound of her voice when she said it. But I did know, without any physical evidence whatsoever, that she would have killed for a draw on a cigarette at that very moment. I also knew she would not light one, never in a million years, with all the sparks of electricity that were floating in the immediate atmosphere. "God, Ray, what is he going to *think*?"

"Who's Ray?" The question ricocheted around the interior of the car. Mr. Jewel Tea's nostrils took a big, whistly breath, but he didn't say a word.

When Dad saw the passenger-side door open, he started down the peeling wooden steps. In a blink, he stood a few steps from my mother, who was half-in and half-out of the car. "Joyce—?"

His question was cut off by the splash of my vomit on the dashboard and windshield. Mom gasped and threw her hands under my chin in time to catch the second retch's worth.

Mr. Jewel Tea moaned. He sounded like he was about to cry. Out of the corner of my eye, I could see him reach for his door handle, stop, roll down his window.

"What's going on?" Dad looked like he'd never seen a car or a kid throwing up before.

"Kenny?" Mom's voice quivered. "It's Carol. She's sick." She held out her vomit-covered hands as if he'd asked her to provide evidence. "Can you help her?" She got herself out of the car without touching anything and wiped her hands on the grass. Before heading for the house, she shot a look of disgust toward the car. I was sure it was aimed at me. My stomach lurched again but nothing came up.

"Aw, bunny, you poor thing." Dad reached toward me but didn't quite seem to know where to put his hands to help me out of the car. "Need help getting out?"

I shook my head, slid toward the door. Other than some on my Keds and in the hair that framed my face, the vomit had done the most damage to Mr. Jewel Tea's car. It ran toward the joint between the windshield and the dash, lodged little bits between the buttons for the radio. My mood lightened as I pictured him with a bucket of water and a toothbrush trying to get it out of the slats of the heater vent.

Dad leaned his head in the car. "Thanks for your help. Let me get a rag and some water so we can get this cleaned up."

I followed Mr. Jewel Tea's eyes to the porch. Mom stood at the top of the steps wiping her hands on a dishtowel watching the car, her spine as straight as a telephone pole.

"No, that's okay." Mr. Jewel Tea's voice sounded like it was trapped in his nose. "You take care of Carol here. Don't worry about this." He had already shifted the car into reverse and was rolling by the time Dad shut the door.

"Well, thanks again," Dad said to the moving car. Mr. Jewel Tea didn't return his wave. "That the principal?"

I shook my head.

"Well, I'm glad it's not *my* car." Dad chuckled and took out a handkerchief, gently cleaned the mess from my hair, mopped the corners of my mouth.

I could feel Mom behind me. She swept my hair off my face and tucked it behind my ears, lightly stroked my cheeks. "Think you're all done throwing up?" Her voice was gentle. Her eyes searched mine. I saw gratitude there. And love.

"Yeah, I'm okay now."

LATENT

adj: present and capable of emerging or developing but not now visible, obvious, active, or symptomatic.

—*Merriam-Webster Dictionary*

It's probably just jock itch," Janeen says after I tell her about the blisters on my dick. I'm in my empty classroom with the door closed talking on the phone during prep time. She laughs and reminds me of the raging rash I developed on our first backpacking trip together. "At least you don't have to hike fifteen miles at altitude."

Trade show sounds in the background alternate with spotty coverage in the convention center to make the conversation halting. She reminds me what my therapist says about perseverating, warns against catastrophizing, then practically yells her treatment advice: "TRY THE LOTRIMIN IN THE MEDICINE CABINET!"

I hope her co-workers have already left for lunch. I remind her my annual checkup happens to be scheduled for this afternoon.

"Good timing."

"Yeah, good timing." I shift in my seat, try not to sound sarcastic.

"Okay, enough about you." She invokes one of our oldest inside jokes. "What about me?"

"What *about* you?"

"Tonight's *Meat Night*." Her voice sounds like Eeyore's, and she makes the *Wha wha wha, Game Over* sound.

Meat Night, the last-night-of-tradeshow ritual that entails dinner and drinks at an expensive steakhouse, where Janeen's boss, Ned, does all the ordering, like a lord over his peons, as she describes it. He makes platters of appetizers appear, orders for the whole sales team whether they like it or not. Ever since he learned Janeen doesn't eat meat, he has taken special pleasure in ordering her the biggest steak on the menu and watching for her reaction when it arrives. By now, she has learned to give him no reaction at all, eat the sides, and give the doggie bag to her beefy sales partner, Henry. Ned still gets a laugh at her expense, nudging whoever is sitting to his right—the top seller of the quarter—getting them to play along with him. Only tonight, Janeen will be the one at his right elbow.

"I love that I finally made it to the top of the chart." She lowers her voice. "But having to sit next to Ned for an entire meal isn't much of a reward."

"Well, congratulations and I'm sorry," I say. "I guess this means no *Daily Show*."

The realization comes with a pang of disappointment. One of the things that gets me through Janeen being away for five, sometimes seven, days at a time is our end-of-evening phone calls, both of us watching the opening of *The Daily Show*, me drinking a beer and wrapped in the fleece Green Bay Packers blanket she made me, Janeen in a hotel bed with a tumbler of wine in a mid-sized city in a different time zone. Hearing her laughing on the other end of the line at exactly the same time I do makes her feel not so far away.

"Well, I've gotta go. Things are starting to pick up here."

I need to get back to work, too. "Okay, I love you."

"I love you, too," she says with an edge of mischief in her voice. "Keep your balls dry!"

THE PAPER UNDER MY THIGHS crinkles loudly as I try to sit up straighter. Pain zings from my balls to my ass, and I tent the gown to create a relieving puff of air. Listen. Nothing. I wiggle my toes to stave off the tingling, check my watch. Thirty minutes. I have been waiting thirty minutes to show the doctor my raw, painful dick.

My fingers itch to text Janeen. She'd set my mind at ease. A knock.

"I'm so sorry to keep you waiting." The doctor balances an open laptop on her forearm while she closes the door behind her. "I really appreciate your patience."

"No worries," my usual answer when I really think the opposite. I shift my weight to my right butt cheek, spread my knees a little farther apart.

"I apologize in advance if we get interrupted. We're waiting for test results for another patient. I told Miranda to let me know the minute they come back."

Again, "No worries."

She places the laptop on the little rolling cart, turns it and her stool to face me, mousing and clicking. "You're here for your annual physical, so let's start with the usual."

My blood pressure looks good. She asks about my bouts of chest pain earlier in the year. Asks if I need any prescriptions renewed, then starts in on all the questions the nurse asked me half an hour ago. Is she testing me? Trying to catch me in a lie? I concentrate to make sure my answers match the earlier ones. Marital status. Number of sexual partners.

I find an opening to tell her about the pain in my groin. This I didn't share with the nurse earlier. What could she do about it anyway?

"Oh, that didn't make it into the notes. Just a sec." The doctor mouses and clicks and types. "When did the pain begin?"

"Sunday. On Saturday, I biked twenty-five miles, and on Sunday, I woke up with this burning sensation all the way down the side of my penis. There's a sore…."

"Okay, let's start with that." She pushes the cart aside and pulls out a ledge for my legs. "You can lie back."

She washes her hands, asks me to lift the gown while she dries them.

Lying down helps, as does the cool air when I lift the gown for her to see. When she does, her hands stop mid-drying. I wish I hadn't looked at her face at just that moment. She probably wishes that, too.

"That's a herpes lesion." She plucks two gloves out of the dispenser. "You haven't had any sexual partners besides your wife?"

I know the answer is no, but my mind starts to race. No, of course not. I haven't slept with anyone else since we got married. Over seven years. A long time. The doctor must sense my discomfort because she stops after putting on the first glove, lays her ungloved hand on my forearm. It's cold. "Your wife then." She says it gently, but it's not a question.

I am about to say, *Of course not.* The possibility of my wife's infidelity has never occurred to me, but now that the doctor has said it aloud, I realize Janeen hasn't been without opportunity.

Beefy Henry jumps into my mind. Marcus at the charity thrift store where she volunteers? The guy at the bread shop who knows her by name?

I look for another explanation. "My wife and I both have occasional cold sores—on our lips." Of course, the doctor knows this. She is the one who wrote the prescription for the huge blue pills in the first place, offered to renew it just a minute ago. "We sometimes have oral sex." Truth is, though,

I can't remember the last time Janeen gave me a blow job or I went down on her.

The doctor shakes her head. It looks like she's trying to come up with a logical answer. "This form of herpes is only sexually—"

A knock. "Doctor?" A voice calls through the door. "I have those results you needed."

The doctor removes her glove and tosses it in the trash receptacle, tosses in the unused one, too.

"I'm so sorry about this. I'll be back as soon as I can. Give that a closer look." And she is gone.

I cover myself with the gown once again. The blister on my penis is actually the least of my pain. Worse is the skin where my thigh meets my groin, under my balls and all the way back to my rectum. Like someone ran a red-hot knife from stem to stern and rubbed salt in it. I breathe and try to focus on the physical pain, so I don't have to deal with the emotional.

Maybe Janeen's infidelity wasn't recent. Maybe before we were married. Herpes can be dormant for a long time. I think. What about the early years when we saw each other only on weekends until I could find a job closer to her?

Of course, if I'm going to go back that far in her sexual history, I have to let myself remember my own cheating at *Pedro's* the summer before we were married, when Janeen had an internship in New York. I have to revisit the dark-haired woman who bought me shot after shot of tequila and told me she'd like some company in her Audi parked out back. She stood then leaving the print of her lush bottom lip smiling at me on her empty shot glass and walked toward the door, the gentle shimmy of her ass under her clingy halter dress confirming she wore no underwear.

I followed her to the red car with Illinois plates and— amazing, considering my level of inebriation—was able to get it up, though not for long. Still, she seemed satisfied and gave me a crinkle-eyed smile as she wiped the lipstick from my mouth with her thumb. "Wouldn't want your girlfriend to see this," she said and then sized up my neck. "Don't know what you're going to do about that though."

In the end, the hickey faded before Janeen returned from New York. I had every intention of coming clean to her about what had happened. She had always been so insistent on our being up front with each other. "If we're going to do the long-distance thing, we need to know that there are no secrets. None!"

I agreed in theory, but in real life, with Janeen's arms around me, the smell of her shampoo filling my nostrils, her pure trust encircling me, I realized there was no way I would tell her. No way I could hurt her by telling her something she would never need to know. The nameless, shot-buying nymphomaniac was long gone. I had learned my lesson, and, best of all, I realized how much I loved Janeen. I proposed the night before she left for her new job. We have been faithful ever since.

At least that's what I thought less than ten minutes ago.

Now everything is upended, and I can't shake the memory of her last return from a business trip. Since she started having to spend so much time on the road, we've followed the same ritual when she returns: no words until we have fallen into bed and reacquainted ourselves with each other's body, light touches on faces, chests, thighs, drinking in the details of all we'd been missing.

But last month, we broke our pattern. She had her period, and it was a heavy one, she said. I didn't have any reason to doubt her.

Still, we took our places on the bed, kissed with our clothes on, walked through notable happenings from our time apart. We opened a bottle of wine, and she told me it had been a tough trip. Ned was a bigger ass than usual, the trade show poorly run. "One giant clusterfuck after another," she said, finished her wine, refilled her glass, and was snoring less than an hour later.

Did she really have her period? Or did she feel too guilty after sleeping with someone else to make love with me? Now that I think of it, we've only made love once since then, and it was less than enthusiastic on her part.

And now my mind is really churning. Maybe it wasn't beefy Henry. Maybe it was someone from a different part of the country all together, Maryland or Montana. Maybe it's the same guy every time. Maybe someone different.

I put my arm across my forehead and try to pay attention to my breathing. 1-2-3-4 counts in. 1-2-3-4 out. Seven years of marriage can't be based on a lie.

My phone buzzes, a text from Janeen: *Good news! Leaving Tampa early. No Meat Night! See you sooooonnnnnn!*

I should be excited, relieved—something—but all I can think about is her betrayal. How will I even look at her when she walks in the door? How will I start the conversation? I play various versions of the scene in my mind. In one, I confront her before she can take off her coat. In another, I pretend like nothing is wrong and give her just enough rope to hang herself. I even consider telling her about what happened at *Pedro's*—beat her to the gut punch. In all of them, we end up divorced, and I end up alone—a lifetime of herpes flair-ups and an inability to trust anyone, ever again. Maybe I won't be there when she gets home. Maybe—

A knock.

I wipe my eyes. "Come in."

The doctor apologizes profusely, leaves the laptop on the cart while she washes her hands again. The furrow in her brow is deeper than before. She says, "You'll never believe—" but then thinks better of it. "Let's just say it's been quite an afternoon."

"No worries."

"So, we're thinking we might have a herpes lesion?"

We? Thinking? Might?!

I lie back. She pulls on gloves and lifts the gown again. "Okay, I'm going to touch."

I hold my breath as she moves my penis left and right, a new kind of agony with each subtle adjustment. I close my eyes.

Please don't touch the inflamed strip. Please.

She guides my knees apart and changes her angle of vision. "Oh, I see."

I hear the snap of gloves being removed.

"You can sit up now."

I push myself back up trying to avoid a zing of pain.

She chucks the glove into the trash can. "The good news is you don't have herpes."

Wait, what?

My ears buzz. The "bad news" comes to me as single words: "shingles" and "antiviral" and "ointment." Something about getting a vaccination.

"I'm sorry if I alarmed you." She makes a funny face. "So. Good. You won't have to have an uncomfortable conversation with your wife tonight."

Tonight.

I try to shake off my conjured scenarios of Janeen's return and replace them with a vision of the two of us rediscovering each other, losing myself in the scent of her hair, stroking the skin on the small of her back softer than velvet, her breath in my ear, our fingers entwined.

Still, the fact that I don't have herpes doesn't explain her extra-heavy periods, her lackluster lovemaking. Henry. Marcus. Maybe some stranger in *Pedro's* for all I know. I try but can't find a way shake the myriad ways she might have betrayed me.

NUMBERED DAYS

Mrs. Morrison was too busy to die. One look at the family calendar would confirm that. Pickups and drop-offs for soccer and dance and 4-H, her kids' volunteer gigs—even organizing carpools to get them to activities took time she didn't have. Throw in a dentist appointment— what?! It seemed like she was there every other month and, of course, she was because somehow the kids' appointments never lined up with hers or each other's. Drop in the ortho- dontist appointments and a cat with blood in her urine. Yes, Mrs. Morrison was much too busy to die. Thank you very much.

One day, looking at the family calendar, she came to a stunning realization: it wouldn't be cancer or stroke that would end up killing her. Not Alzheimer's as she had long suspected. No, Mrs. Morrison would simply be done in by her calendar.

This made sense. Somewhere she'd read that everyone's heart had only a certain number of beats in it. If you spent your life overweight and out of shape, you used up your heartbeats much more quickly than someone with a slow and steady pulse. What if the same were true of your life cal- endar? What if you were allotted a finite number of entries?

She sat down at her computer and took stock of the color-coded calendar that appeared on the screen. Nine entries dedicated to carpools in the last week alone, nine entries squandered on moving bodies from here to there, for goodness' sake. She looked for evidence that she was more than a part-time chef and full-time driver—oh and a part-time librarian, which was her "real job" as her kids called it with air quotes. There it was: six months earlier she'd gotten her hair cut and highlighted. And she went to book club once a month. But how many entries had she made for her painting? In the last twelve months: none. Oh, sure, she'd painted some but only little snatches between tasks on the calendar, nothing that got scheduled like those darned dental appointments or cleaning the dishwasher filter. For god's sake, she had wasted calendar entries on cleaning the dishwasher filter!

So it was that on May 5th, Mrs. Morrison decided she'd had enough with this electronic calendar and its rainbow of responsibilities. She bought a black day planner with pristine white pages. The calendar had both month-at-a-glance and week-at-a-glance pages with big sections for adding detail. She decided, however, that her entries would be simple: "Paint" with a nice long arrow running from one o'clock, when she got home from work, to four o'clock when the kids got off the bus.

She envisioned herself painting in the little studio space she'd set up in the extra bedroom, the space that had long ago become piled with clothes to be mended, winter gear to organize and put away, and, inexplicably, a single hockey skate. Neither kid played hockey. Oh yes, she'd planned to plant a couple of zinnias in it and give it to her brother for his front porch. Help him spruce things up after his wife left him. Pulling the skate out of the neighbor's trash had been as far as she'd gotten.

But none of that mattered. Tomorrow, she would clear out her studio space. *May 6th: Clear Studio from 1:00–3:00.* And because she could, because the paper planner gave her room for it, she created sub-tasks: *Mending: 1:00–2:00. Winter Gear: 2:00–3:00*—then erased them. She would *not* waste entries on sub-tasks. The decks cleared, she would still have an hour left to paint before the kids got home.

But, wait, wasn't May 6th a Thursday? The day school let out a half-hour early. Thursday was also Mrs. Morrison's day to drive carpool for dance. She would pick up her daughter at school and get a snack into her before they headed out. Before that, though, Mrs. Morrison would also need to make a meal that her daughter could eat in the car on the way home, so she could get right to her homework when they walked through the door. Last time she'd forgotten this task, Mrs. Morrison had found herself reheating leftovers and making a salad at 9:00.

Why Mrs. Morrison took the task of getting her family fed to be a mark of her suitability as a mother, she'd never been able to determine. Perhaps because she'd given up a perfectly good career to stay home and now was unable to find more than part-time employment that barely paid minimum wage. Thank goodness for her husband's union job at the printing company. Still, because *she* wasn't bringing in much money, perhaps she felt she could earn her keep by seeing that her children were nutritiously fed. A therapist would have a field day with that, but, since there wasn't space on the calendar for an appointment, this would have to wait until the kids were in college—when she would also be able to start painting again. Painting! Yes, she would add that to the calendar.

She was tempted to write "Paint!" on the time slots while her daughter would be dancing, but she knew that was just plain silly. She couldn't drag her supplies into the youth arts building and just set up the easel. Why wasn't she a writer? You could do that anywhere! She'd probably be on her third novel by now with all the time she spent waiting for lessons and practices to end. Yes, in the next life, she would become a writer. Decision made.

By the time they'd get home from dance, there would be just enough time to tidy up, check in with her son, have a glass of wine with her husband and fall asleep watching a TV show. Okay, May 6th was out.

May 7th, though, that had real promise.

On the one o'clock line, she wrote in nice, bold letters: P-A-I-N—Before she could finish the word, however, the calendar exploded, and the shock stopped Mrs. Morrison's heart.

ONLY ONE

I'll do what I can," I find myself saying to the woman on the other end of the phone, though I'm not sure what I have agreed to. I sit up. Try to focus my eyes. The clock reads 4:03. a.m.? p.m.?

"Oh, that's wonderful!"

P.M. I must have nodded off.

"Little Caroline will love being your assistant, and, most importantly, we'll raise lots of money for our *Make a Wish* project. We're sending her to the Wisconsin Dells. See you Saturday." And she's gone.

Assistant? I check the notes scribbled on a pad. Apparently, I have agreed to have "Little Caroline" assist in my *Illusionist for Jesus* show this Saturday at Grace Life Bible Church. But I work alone. Always have. As I start to call back Mrs. Tredwell and tell her so, though, my mother's voice rings in my head. "Beggars can't be choosers, Allan." Her voice blends with that of my deceased mentor, Rolando the Great—real name Jerry—"You gotta take the money where you make the money." This aphorism allowed Jerry, a dyed-in-the-wool atheist, to build a thriving business doing magic tricks for dyed-in-the-wool Christians, grateful to have a wholesome form of entertainment for their kids' birthdays and first communion parties.

On Saturday, parents will drop off their kids while they shop at the church's craft bazaar. I'll do tricks loosely connected to Bible stories and take home my first paycheck in four weeks. And, somehow, work "Little Caroline" into the show. I guess.

ON PERFORMANCE DAY, my supply-organizing ritual calms me. Rings, handcuffs, trick boxes, silk scarves, decks of cards. I find a trick that will include Caroline: the box for sawing off her hand. I buff the mirror inside with a soft cloth, use mineral oil on the saw blade.

As I run through my lines, I fold my cape, and place it with my top hat in my rolling cart. "Now, remember, boys and girls, what I do are tricks, illusions. Only one person can do real magic, or more precisely, miracles—"

I hold up one finger both to emphasize the "one" and to turn their eyes heavenward. "Who is that?" I always ask.

Some say, "God!" Others, "Jesus!"

I don't quibble. I have lost track of which denominations give credit to God and which to Jesus. That's their thing, and I leave them to it.

After one more run-through, I prepare to lift my shield, a vital part of preparation. When I was in high school, my therapist concluded I was unable to feel empathy or compassion. Too literal, he said. Today, they'd put me on the autism spectrum.

Truth is, I pick up on every emotion floating around a room. The good ones, yes, but mostly the unpleasant ones. Guilt. Jealousy. Fear. In fact, even at age sixteen, I felt how desperately the therapist needed to be right about my lack of empathy, so I let him think he was right. I have spent my whole life building defenses, dulling the sensations that permeate a room. I make it appear I feel nothing at all. The Illusionist isn't me.

Or maybe he is.

I close my eyes and picture a plexiglass tube ascending around me from the floor. I reach out my right index finger, give it a tap directly in front of my nose, and it turns into a golden gel that folds itself comfortably around me, holding me securely, hardening in a way that allows natural movement without any fissures.

To get me through, I remind myself to anticipate something after the gig. I'll treat myself to some PBS time. It isn't Popcorn Day, but I'll make an exception and pop a big batch. I'm already letting Caroline into the show. I might as well break routine in honor of popcorn. Maybe it's like in math class: two negatives equal a positive.

When I arrive at the church, Mrs. Tredwell shows me to the fellowship hall and thanks me three times for working Caroline into the show. As I set up, she reminds me—again three times—not to call what I do "magic." She has forgotten this language is written straight into the contract. Some people can never be too careful.

When I ask to meet Caroline, Mrs. Tredwell refuses. "We want her to be surprised. The photographer wants to catch her expression when you call her up on stage."

"Do you think that's a good idea?" Sometimes people get stage fright.

"Oh, you don't know Little Caroline. She'll be fine."

Popcorn, I tell myself. Popcorn.

Children's voices interrupt us. Mrs. Tredwell ushers me off to a closet. She doesn't want them to see me. "That would ruin the effect."

Do you want me to appear magical or human? I can't figure people out.

"Sorry, there's no light."

I settle in and leave the door open a crack. Maybe I'll see Caroline.

Some children settle on the floor in front of my performance area, while their parents stand at the back of the room. The bazaar probably hasn't opened yet.

Despite my shield, I can feel the collective anticipation of the children, excitement and fear of the unknown. The promise and threat of surprise.

Soon, the room is filled, and Mrs. Tredwell comes into the closet for more chairs. I give her mine, slip into a corner, and fluff my cape. I recognize a low hum—like the buzz of a beehive so pervasive you don't find you're hearing it until you see the cloud of bees and realize the sound has been in your ears all along.

The sounds hush and a microphone emits its obligatory whine. Mrs. Tredwell welcomes the audience and goes through my bio. It includes only the pertinent details, training at Pendleton Prestidigitation Academy, membership in the Society of American Illusionists, my apprenticeship with Rolando the Great. I leave out the time spent at the Institution. Irrelevant.

Mrs. Tredwell is contract-bound to stick to the introduction as I have written it, so I can time my entrance just right. After the line about my coming all the way from the Far East (pause) side of Antigo (laughs from parents), she is supposed to say, "Boys and girls, moms and dads, I give you, Master Illusionist, The Amazing Allan!" On the final word, my cape gets a big flourish. I step forward majestically and take a deep bow, at which point, the audience sees a message taped to the top of my hat that says, *Are you ready to be amazed?*

However, just as I am about to open the closet door, I hear words I have not written, an explanation of "why we are here," the amount of money needed to make Caroline's dream come true, and other details that embarrass the parents and douse the children's enthusiasm. Mrs. Tredwell has talked herself into a spiral and doesn't know how to get out of it. The hazard of going off script.

Before things can get worse, I step onto the performance area behind her, put my finger to my lips, and pretend to creep up on her as if this uncomfortable moment is part of the show. Children put their hands to their mouths, giggle. I mime that I am about to make Mrs. Tredwell disappear on the count of three and start making exaggerated finger gestures. The children whisper, "One," and "Two," and then explode on the number, "Three!"

I pull myself directly in front of Mrs. Tredwell with my arms up, holding my cape to block her from the audience's view. Quickly, we walk toward stage right allowing her to slink away and blend in with the parents standing along the wall.

I wait one beat before whipping around with a gigantic smile on my face, my eyebrows dancing. A burst of applause. I have gotten them back.

As I make my way through the warm-up tricks, I scan the crowd trying to figure out which child is Caroline. By trick number five, I am pretty sure it's the blonde, blue-eyed waif at the front, with her large eyes and pale complexion. She watches with the intentness of an art collector examining a Renoir.

I ask for an assistant, but she keeps her hand down. I reach mine toward her. "You, dear?"

Her expression remains unchanged, but she stands, takes my hand.

I have brought along my childhood cape, the first my mother ever made me, and tie it around her shoulders. Fabric pools on the floor. I place my child-sized top hat on her head and whisper, "Don't be afraid, Caroline, the crowd will love you."

She whispers something back, but I can't hear it. I notice Mrs. Tredwell out of the corner of my eye looking nervous.

"Boys and girls, let's say hello to—"

"Madeline."

I kick myself for every decision that has led to this off-script moment. I grab a deck of cards. Popcorn, I repeat to myself. Popcorn.

"Thanks for being my *first* assistant today, Madeline!"

With my emphasis on the word, *first*, Mrs. Tredwell's shoulders relax.

I lead Madeline through an *I can guess your card* trick that nearly does her in, what with all the eyes on her and this strange man telling her to pick cards and remember them. Halfway through, she has forgotten the card—not as unusual as you might think—so I segue into a let's-make-your-card-jump trick.

By the time she pulls the ace of diamonds from the back of her hatband and shows it to the audience, to peals of laughter and applause, her nervousness has dissipated.

"You've done it, Madeline. You're a magician!"

Too late. I have used the wrong term. I could be strung up as a heretic, but the relief on her face makes the slip worth it.

"Can I get a round of applause for my assistant, Madeline?"

While she returns to her spot, I pull out the climax trick and leave nothing to chance. "Okay. Is there anyone here named Caroline?"

A camera flashes. All heads turn toward a little girl at the side of the room, her face the color of ash. She wears a stocking cap pulled down to her eyebrows. How could I have missed her?

As her mother guides her forward, I regret the trick I have chosen. What kind of jerk pretends to cut off the arm of a sick little girl? At the same time, what kind of person would think it a good idea to put her in front of a room full of people to do a trick with a stranger? I blame Mrs. Tredwell.

Her mother pulls Caroline's cap from her head and attempts to fluff the girl's hair, so filled with electricity it clings to her head like a science experiment. The mother looks deeply into Caroline's eyes. Her gaze says every moment with this ailing daughter is a gift and she'll miss the girl desperately when she is gone. I have been in the presence of many mother-daughter pairs, but I have never felt such deep love before. I certainly never felt this from my own mother. I have lost my edge.

Shield compromised.

Nothing to do but keep going. Caroline looks up at me. I lead her to her mark.

"Which hand do you color with, honey?" She holds up her left. "Okay, then, we'd better remove this one." I point to her right. "Don't worry," I say, "I've never lost a right hand." I turn to the audience and stage whisper, "Yet!"

The eyes of the kids in front row get big. The adults laugh politely.

I continue with the usual spiel showing that the box is solid, the saw is real. I let a kid examine it.

Caroline sits patiently. I ask her to give me her right hand, so I can place it in the box. The moment I touch her, I can feel her need, an electric current beneath her skin. Her eyes grab mine and she whispers, "Please use your magic to fix me."

She starts to say something about her mother, but I can't hear it over my lines.

"When I first started doing this trick, I had to send a few assistants to a second-hand store!" I make the ba-dah-bum sound. The parents groan. The kids laugh though they don't know why.

Caroline grips my hand inside the box, and, in her touch, I feel such desperation I say the second thing I shouldn't. "Don't worry, honey, my magic can fix anything."

HALFWAY THROUGH MY BOWL of oatmeal the next day, the phone rings. Mrs. Tredwell.

"You have broken your contract. Worse yet, you have given false hope to a little girl and greatly upset her parents. Who do you think—" Her voice is so charged with anger, I try to raise my shield and repress the urge to remind her the contract was broken the moment she went off script during my intro. You think I have to walk a babbling woman off stage every day? Instead, let her go on.

When she pauses to take a breath, I interject, "Perhaps she misunderstood. Kids sometimes get swept up in the show. Think they see and hear things that aren't there. I am an illusionist after all." I can feel her anger dissipate, not because she believes my explanation but because she now has one for Caroline's parents. "Tell them that," I say.

I resist the urge to add, 'Or tell them she *won't* get better. Would that make them happy?' But, even as I think the words, I am visited by the realization that Caroline *will* get better. Inexplicably, she'll go on to play violin professionally and live a long happy life with her partner and a series of dogs named after obscure composers.

I also know, somehow, her recovery is due to me.

I CONTINUE TO TAKE EVERY GIG I CAN GET—Vacation Bible School, the Crossroads Church Fall Festival, Prayer-Pa-Looza in Algoma. They go fine. In fact, in some ways, I feel as if I am approaching my zenith performance-wise, like the proverbial machine firing on all cylinders. Still, the shows feel hollow after healing Caroline.

Although it has been years since I've made a cold call, I phone Holy Redeemer Senior Home, hungry to see if I can work my healing magic on someone else. Everyone in the place is knocking on death's door, so what's to be lost?

When performance day arrives, I brace myself for a less involved audience than I'm used to with kids. It must be a good time of day. The patients seem lively. Maybe their meds haven't kicked in yet. Or maybe they have.

By and large, the oldies seem to get the wonder of my illusions. Sensitive to the patients' difficulty in tracking long, involved tricks—and knowing that their minds are doing the most amazing tricks of all—I keep the illusions simple, make sure to give an extra flourish to cue when to "ooo" and "aahhh" and clap.

While talking through my tricks, I scan the room considering who might need my healing touch. Off to the side sits a woman, younger than the others. She is dressed neatly in beige slacks, a powder pink top with a matching cardigan. Her hands rest in her lap.

I must be careful how I request an assistant, or I'll end up with the old lady in the front row who keeps muttering things under her breath like, "That's an easy one. Didn't you see the extra coin in his other hand?" and "I could do that..." and then giving away the trick of the trick.

Breaking with my usual procedure, I loosen my shield and leave the front of the room—pulling coins from male patients' ears and offering silk flowers pulled from my apparently empty hand to a few of the ladies. I stop in front of the pink sweater lady who I now think of as Brenda. "Ma'am, would you be so kind as to help me with my next trick?" She takes my hand, despite her obvious confusion. A current flows between us. The healing has begun.

"Can I get a round of applause for my lovely assistant?" Normally, I would make small talk about her job or the weather. "I bet you have a lovely singing voice. Any chance you could sing a song to help the coin move from my right hand to my left?"

She starts to sing, "You Are My Sunshine..." Flawless. People in the audience, whose eyes looked vacant and confused just a moment ago, now are alert, engaged.

"Please don't take my sunshine away."

My work is done. By year's end, her doctors will have written their white paper titled, "The Effects of Light Therapy in Conjunction with a Glucose-Free Diet on Early Onset Dementia: A Case Study." Brenda's husband, who'd had feelings for his assistant even before Brenda's dementia was diagnosed, will make the difficult decision to stay with his wife, while financially supporting his fifth child unbeknownst to Brenda. To the assistant's credit, she will go to her grave asserting that the child was the product of a one-night stand with a traveling salesman.

AFTER I STOP USING MY SHIELD all together, my business takes off, and I become selective about the jobs I accept, making sure to work gigs where there's a strong likelihood of someone needing a cure. Children's hospitals and fundraisers for a childhood diseases are the best. Soon, I realize that in every crowd there are myriad ailments—some as yet undi-agnosed—like the woman who wanders in from a wedding reception in the ballroom down the hall. Her abdomen is filled with a cancer that she and her doctor have unknowingly kept masked with painkillers for "fibroids." I do some fancy footwork to choose her as an assistant over the kids raising their hands. But this woman needs my help, first to drive out the cancer then to kick the opioid addiction, which turns out to be just as aggressive as The Big C.

I continue to recite my mantra. "What I do are tricks and illusions. The only one who can do real magic is…" I point one finger toward heaven, though now I tilt it slightly toward myself, too.

As time goes on, though, each performance takes a little more out of me. I need longer to build up enough energy for the next show. Soon I start to hear whisperings. "He cured a little girl with Muscular Dystrophy over in Muscoda." True. "He restored the foot of a soldier who stepped on an IED." Not true. "He reversed a vasectomy and the guy's wife got pregnant." Who knows?

People elbow each other out of the way, so they can shove their kids at me. Even kids with nothing wrong with them at all. Maybe the parents think I can protect them from future calamities. Never underestimate the desperation of parents.

Despite the surge of power I feel with each performance, I also remember what happened to the last guy who healed people and performed miracles.

AS I LEAVE WHAT I VOW will be my last healing, a woman waits at my minivan. While I load my things into the back, she tells the story of Sydney, her granddaughter, the victim of a drunk driver, paralyzed. Brain dead. Sydney's mother, April, is a complete mess because, well, she was the drunk driver.

This one I don't want to touch with a twelve-foot pole, and I should tell her so, but the post-healing let-down is starting to set in. My limbs are heavy, and I'm having trouble keeping my eyes open. I need to get home. "Here's my card. Call me tomorrow."

Unfortunately, my healing-hangover lasts longer than usual, and sometime in the next 72 hours, I apparently take Grandma's call and write her name and "Holy Blood of Our Savior Church" on my calendar. "No hospital. Go directly to church."

Of course, I could cancel but decide, Why not? It's not like Sydney will be any worse off. The feeling of invincibility begins its pre-healing ascent.

THE MOMENT I WALK INTO the room off the vestibule, it is obvious this performance is going to be different. No pretense of a magic show. No kids.

A whispered, "You're here. May God bless you." The grandmother.

The room has a single hospital bed in the middle with a soft light illuminating Sydney who can't be older than fifteen. How did they get her here? In this bed? And the monitor over her left shoulder? The urine bag under the sheet? People—twenty-three of them, hands folded, heads bowed—ring the room in the shadows. A woman sits on a chair next to the bed, her wrung-out face and stringy hair leaving no question as to her relationship to the girl.

"This is April." The grandmother guides my hands to April's. At our touch, her desperation shoots up my arms straight to the pain center of my brain. The accident, tires screaming, metal crumpling, glass exploding. Silence. Long minutes until the peal of a siren slices the air. Thwap, thwap, thwap of Flight for Life.

The grandmother neglected to tell me about the death of the other car's driver, that April is out on bail and awaiting trial, that even if I heal Sydney, everything will not be all right. Not by a long shot.

I want to tell her this, tell her the truth. But the collective hope of the people in the room holds me in place. I must at least give them the impression of a healing. Some measure of hope.

"Please move in closer. Hold each other's hands and make a circle." I know this will have no real effect, but they believe it will. That is what matters.

When the final hand is grasped, Sydney opens her eyes and the room gasps. It is all I can do not to recoil. The girl's brokenness is like another presence in the room. Her eyes stare straight at me, but I know they cannot see. They close again.

I place my top hat upon her abdomen and drop a coin inside. Cover the hat with a red silk scarf and say the hocus pocus words on her behalf.

The people hum. "Amazing Grace."

Of course.

I want to silence them, so I can concentrate, but their power to heal is stronger than mine. I know this.

I can't tell if these people believe in the miracle of tran-substantiation—an eerie trick that turns a thin cracker and slurp of wine into flesh and blood to atone for their sins—but judging from the fear and self-loathing that permeates the room, I'd say yes. For all I know, along with the blight of Original Sin, they shoulder responsibility for Sydney and April's calamity, too. Perhaps, in their eyes, God is punishing them all. Who knows?

They hum the final notes of the hymn and start in again from the top. I pick up Sydney's hands. Nothing. Holding them over the hat, I say a few nonsense words then settle her arms back at her sides, signal that my work here is done. The others finish the measure they are on, the one about once being blind and now being able to see.

Unlike other performances where I leave assured that the healing is underway, I put my hat on my head knowing not only that Sydney has not been healed today, but she will die of pneumonia three months hence, a demise that some will silently trace back to having her moved to the church for my failed miracle. Though they'll silently blame me, they won't go so far as to call for my crucifixion. They also don't know that at the exact moment of Sydney's passing, April will be entering her plea of no contest to manslaughter or that the prosecutor will later show mercy and not bring the second charge for the death of her daughter.

"When will she come around?" The grandmother's eyes are clear, her expression trusting.

I point my finger upward. "Only one..."

PAY PHONE

1

The dime rolled off the tip of Deena's finger into the slot, clinked through the contraption's insides. A click, then a dial tone. Thank God, she wouldn't be stuck in the dark school with the creepy janitor, Mr. Lightner, until her mother came out of her reading fog and realized she'd forgotten to pick up her daughter from 4-H Club. Last time, it had taken two hours for the mists of her romance novel to lift. When her mother's car appeared in front of the school, Deena had sobbed like a baby.

Now, she dialed her grandfather's number, waited. Two rings. Three rings. Four. How long could a phone ring without someone answering it? She had no idea.

"Hello." The voice was male but not her grandfather's. "Potter residence. Jerry speaking."

Her shoulders dropped. "Sorry, wrong number."

Her only dime.

2
ABC

"C'MON. C'MON. GIVE ME FIFTEEN CENTS." The phone book was open to the P's. Mr. Randolph Plunkett would soon receive the funniest prank call of the century.

Deena's best friend, Barb, fished coins out of her jeans pocket, dropped them into the slot.

Over the past two days, they'd made calls to Mr. Plunkett from Barb's house and asked if his refrigerator was running.

"I think so," had come his innocent response.

"Well, you'd better go catch it!" They could hardly contain their laughter. This guy: how did he fall for that not once but twice? Maybe he was lonely.

By today, surely, he'd have gotten wise.

Deena disguised her voice hoping to make it manly. "Hello, Mr. Plunkett. This is MG&E. There has been an outage in your neighborhood. Could you please check to see if your refrigerator is running?" She covered the mouthpiece, so he couldn't hear them laughing.

"Very funny. In fact, my refrigerator *isn't* running. How do ya like them apples?"

She didn't bother to change her voice now. "Well, you'd better go Plunkett in!" She pinched her knees together, so she wouldn't pee her pants.

The best fifteen cents they'd ever spent.

3
DEF

"MAKE SURE YOU HAVE A QUARTER with you, Deena." This was her mother's version of feminism: if a woman's date started pushing in a direction that she was unwilling to go, she could just take that quarter, find a pay phone, and get herself a taxi, thank you very much. An elegant solution that had served her mother well in the years before she'd met her husband.

Of course, her mother had never encountered a man like Charlie.

4
GHI

A ringing came from the back of the store. A telephone? The one next to the cash register was silent. Ah, the pay phone next to the soda cooler. Her customer seemed not to hear it even as it started in on its fourth ring. Was he deaf? She slid his cigarettes into a bag. "Thanks. Come again."

The ringing drowned out the bell over the door when he left. Wrong number, probably. Soon they would give up.

Deena looked around the store. She was alone—alone except for the ringing, which showed no sign of letting up, though what that "sign" would be, she couldn't say. She looked at the clock. Three more hours until her shift would be over. The ringing needed to stop. Right. Now.

She made her way down the candy aisle, considered lifting the receiver and dropping it right back into its cradle. Changed her mind, said, "Hello?"

"Heavenly mercy, you answered!" The woman's voice quavered. "I was afraid I had disappeared completely."

How many times had Deena felt the same thing? Charlie had that effect on her.

"I—" The voice on the phone was a whisper. "I'm real. Right?"

Deena held up her hand in front of her face to be sure she could still see it.

"Right?" The voice was desperate.

"Yes," she answered, though she didn't really know for sure. "Yes, you're real."

5
JKL

THE OPERATOR'S VOICE WAS TINNY and impatient. "Ma'am, I *said*, will you accept the charges?"

Silence on the other end.

"Come on, Ma, just accept the charges." Deena could hardly choke out the words. Why had she left the apartment without her purse? A collect call had been her only choice. She pictured Charlie passed out on the couch by now. Maybe she could sneak back in—

"Yes, I'll accept."

A click and then the operator's voice. "Go ahead."

More silence.

How could Deena describe everything that had gone down with Charlie? His explosiveness. His ability to make her feel so small. She took a long, slow, deep breath and held it until her lungs hurt.

Her mother sighed on the other end. "Have you had enough then?"

6
MNO

EVERY DAY, SHE PASSED the phone booth on her way to and from class, but today was different. Today, she felt strong. She'd take the high road—wish Charlie a happy birthday, tell him he could keep her records and her favorite mug. Tell him she was real. Soon, she'd have her GED and a ticket to a four-year college. No hard feelings.

The first ring felt like validation.

The second like victory.

Numbers three, four, and five felt increasingly dangerous. Was it her imagination, or did the length of each trill get longer than the one before?

Seven.

Eight.

Nine.

She fished the busines card her mother had given her from the side pocket of her backpack. *Samantha Mills, Therapist, MSW, LCSW.* That would be a better use of her fifty cents.

She pressed the silver lever to end the call.

Wait! Had she heard the click of his picking up?

Change jingled through the phone's insides and landed in the coin slot. Enough for another call.

7
PRS

HER FLIGHT WOULD GET IN two hours late. Perfect. Just perfect. No, she couldn't deplane during the emergency layover in Tulsa. No, there was no way to get word to her potential new employer that she would be late for the interview. She checked in with each muscle in her body. Yup, tight as a harp string.

She knew better than to accept the pill offered by the man next to her—"The yellow ones help me in times like these"—but she took it anyway. Same for the complimentary glass of wine. And a second. Or was that a third?

In Terminal B, after wandering around in circles for a while, she found a pay phone, pushed the buttons. The notes of the firm's number sounded uncannily like "California, Here I Come." She sang along. When she got to the line, "A sun kissed miss said, 'Don't be late!'" she belted it out like a jazz singer, missed the voice on the other end saying, "Hanson, Roland & Donovan, may I help you? Hello?"

She stopped singing and explained her situation.

"You're in luck," said the receptionist. The last interview of the day had cancelled. "We'll send a car for you right now."

8
TUV

DEENA FOLLOWED THE BLUE LINE on the floor from the elevator to the bank of telephones near the front entrance of the hospital and chose the one at the very end. She was grateful to her mother for keeping a small address book in her purse and to the EMTs or the police or whoever had thought to grab it from the mangled car and bring it to the hospital.

She fished the long-distance calling card from her wallet and started punching in numbers. It had been years since

she'd talked to Aunt Maggie, her relationship with her aunt—
or, rather, lack of it—collateral damage in the estrangement
between the two older women. Deena never did find out
what had caused the rift but was grateful for her mother's
desire to set things right. Silver linings for a near fatal wreck.

"Hello." Her aunt's voice sounded exactly like her mother's. "You have reached Margaret Logan's answering machine.
Please leave a message at the beep."

Deena prattled on about the accident trying to lay a foun-
dation for healing between the sisters but ran out of tape
before she could get to the point.

9
WXY

"DEENIE? IT'S CHARLIE DON'T HANG UP I only have a few
minutes before the next guy gets the phone I'm getting sober
can you believe it? and I'm calling to say I'm sorry it's part
of my treatment program apologizing owning it making
amends they say it's important to be clear about what we're
apologizing for even though a lot of it I don't remember so
I'll just say I'm sorry for all the times I drank too much and
ran you down I'm starting to see I did that because I felt so
bad about myself and if I could make you feel lower than
me then I wasn't the lowest you know? and I don't expect
us to be friends or anything but I feel bad about hurting
you and hope you have a good life and…and…and…yeah,
okay, I gotta go 'bye."

0
OPER

SHE SHOULD HAVE KNOWN BETTER than to let her co-worker
set her up with a guy whose vanity license plate was FSHS-
LYR. What could have made Laura think Deena would hit
it off with someone like that? Forty-five minutes straight of

him, him, him. In another life, she would have hung around to see how it would play out.

Instead, she signaled the server for a to-go box and drained her margarita. It had been a stroke of genius to tell her date she needed to keep her phone on in case her mother needed her. If only the battery hadn't died.

She held up her finger, pretending to see a call coming in on her phone's dark screen. "It's Mom." She stood, grabbed her purse, and headed for the door, willing him not to follow.

The pay phone in the restaurant's entrance was long gone. Same with the booth that had been on the corner and the one in front of the library two blocks down. She imagined them like butterflies emerging from their cocoons in the night, leaving behind their glass and aluminum casings whose doors rarely closed completely, pinched fingers when they did. Even a quarter wouldn't help her now.

She approached the nice-looking man in front of the bookstore. "Pardon me, my cell died." She showed him the inert phone. "Could I trouble you to call me a taxi?"

PRETTY PEOPLE

Keith Riordan was terrible with the camera, at least that's what he wanted people to believe. He wanted them to think it was his ineptness and poor timing that yielded such terrible driver's license pictures. He wanted them to think he would do better if only he could.

Only, he *could*.

He knew how to snap the shutter a split-second before their smile became wooden, how to get them to tilt their chin to avoid "turkey neck." He even could, when he wanted to, make people look a touch better than they did in real life. Only he hadn't wanted to for a good long while.

Sure, his little work hobby would probably register somewhere on the pathetic scale, but he also couldn't seem to stop taking crummy headshots of the people who came to his station at the DMV. He even took some pride in the unflattering and downright ugly images that would later identify their subjects in routine traffic stops, when they bought a bottle of wine, or had to show ID to vote.

Maybe it was a power thing. The power to remind others that they had just as many imperfections as he did. And the ones who needed the most reminding were those with the best hair, the highest cheekbones, the straightest teeth. The Pretty People.

He'd see one coming and get a flutter in his chest. "Please put your toes on the line," he'd say. "I'll tell you when to smile." Only he wouldn't. He'd snap the picture a split-second *before* he gave the signal or a heartbeat *after*. He gave himself extra points when he caught a woman with her tongue unflatteringly underneath her upper lip trying to swab away errant lipstick. He labeled these *The Chimps* and numbered each one before he forwarded the .jpg to his personal email address to laugh at it later.

But the most fun were the men, *The Chumps*, with their strong jawlines, their straight noses, their hair that fell just right. They had features that would never show in the photograph: bulging pecs, narrow hips, hands that could do some damage. The more of those traits, the more unforgiving his camera. Keith would catch his subjects looking constipated or as if they were letting a rather loud fart. Sometimes, both.

One Friday afternoon after a particularly long dry spell with no Pretty People, Keith looked at the next name in his queue. Alex Blount. Alex Blount? The name grabbed him by the throat. *The* Alex Blount from high school? The Alex Blount who got the great job at the biotech startup on the West Coast and never came back? The Alex Blount who'd touched Keith's ass once in Chemistry class then pretended it didn't happen?

Keith scanned the waiting area. An old lady whose knees splayed out at odd angles. A young mother balancing a toddler on her hip while she helped her other kid stick a straw into a juice box. A nervous-looking teenager and his equally nervous-looking mother. A rosy-faced bald guy wearing a fluorescent yellow safety vest and dusty jeans. Maybe that was him, Alex Blount, *Sr.* Of course.

Keith added the "Sr" designation to his information and motioned him over. "Mr. Blount? I can take you now."

The man didn't look up from cleaning his fingernails.

Keith called louder. "Mr. Blount? Alex Blount?"

"Coming!" a throaty woman's voice called from the restroom area around the corner.

Keith squinted at the construction worker. His daughter, maybe?

"Here I come!" A woman rounded the corner hoisting a huge handbag on her shoulder. Her clicking steps sounded like the rat-a-tat of a machine gun.

The instant he saw her bleached hair, her heavy though tasteful makeup, her undulating breasts, and her jeans so tight he could see the bulge of her keys in her front pocket, he knew his dry spell was over. Finally, a Pretty Person.

"Here I am. Sorry," she puffed, "where do you want me?"

"Alex Blount?" He said it as a question, but now he could see, there was no question at all. Cut and dye the hair, lose the makeup, flatten those breasts, and there was Alex. He had always worn skin-tight jeans, only then his bulge was front and center. Keith slid the clipboard down to cover the beginnings of his unbidden erection.

"The one and only!" She—he?—dropped the handbag next to the background screen and stepped to the line. "Here, right?"

"Uhm. Yes. There. Yes."

Click. Hover. Click. He couldn't look directly at Alex's image on the screen. The heat of shame made its way up his neck—for himself, yes, but also for Alex. How could he go out in public like that? Have that girl-face on his driver's license? Didn't he care that people were laughing at him? Keith looked around the waiting room. No one was laughing. No one else seemed to notice the guy dressed up like a girl, pretending to be something he wasn't.

Alex cleared his throat. "Uhm?"

"Oh, yeah." Keith snapped the picture. "You can have a seat over there. They'll call your name when your license is ready."

THAT EVENING, KEITH POWERED up his laptop, fidgeted while he waited. So Alex hadn't recognized him. And why would he? The last time they'd been together, Keith was seventy pounds lighter, had a full head of hair and a case of acne that required the highest dose of Accutane the dermatologist had ever prescribed. Not to mention the fact that they had never really run in the same circles anyway. Circles? Huh. Charlie Mulroy and Becca Petersen could hardly be considered a *circle*, more like a small triangle of misfits who geeked out on video games in Keith's basement on Saturday nights.

Alex, on the other hand, always had more friends than you could count. Most of them in the drama club, one more flamboyant than the next. In fact, Alex had seemed to be the most mainstream of them all, always carrying off lead roles, *male* lead roles, with such believability no one would have doubted which team he played for. He went on to study computer science, for god's sake.

Keith would never have questioned Alex's preferences if not for the stray hand at the lab table their junior year. The immediate and forceful *shwing* that followed the touch, made Keith doubt his own sexuality. The *shwing* would return every time Keith thought about the incident for weeks afterwards.

In the moment, Keith told himself the touch had been inadvertent—then why no "Excuse me" or "Sorry, dude?" Instead, Alex just placed the beaker on the counter, continued checking off items on the equipment list. Keith tried to comfort himself with the notion that his boner had been caused by a glimpse of Stephanie Dahl's fine ass as she leaned over the lab table in front of him.

And here it was again—mild but present—as he looked at the photograph on his screen. The picture of the new Alex gazed back at him, a truly perfect picture of a Pretty Person. Hair smooth, just the right head tilt, cute left dimple. The camera had even managed to catch eyelight. Now if *she* had touched his ass, he'd have had to be gay *not* to get hard.

Keith created a new file, titled it (ALEX) and dragged the New Alex's picture into it. Funny, he had saved all the other photos so diligently—giving them each unique names and numbers and organizing them by category—yet, once they were tucked safely into their files, he rarely went back and looked at them. As if just knowing they were there was enough. In fact, the few times he'd gotten curious and clicked on a random one for a laugh, the sight of the person's face created a twinge of sadness. And in that twinge, he'd push away thoughts about what kind of loser makes himself feel better by making others look bad.

"GUESS WHO'S BACK IN TOWN?" Keith hadn't planned to share the news of Alex's return, but an hour and a half of gaming and a few beers loosened his tongue.

Charlie's eyes stayed glued to the screen. "Who." He didn't sound interested enough to make the word a question. "Die, you mother!"

"Alex Blount."

"Who."

"Blount. Alex Blount. From high school. You know the guy in all the plays? He dated Georgia Rimes."

"Don't remember either of them." Charlie took a swallow of beer. "He's back. So what."

"Man, this is weird." Keith paused, hoping Charlie would stop playing, show some interest. None. "He's not a *he* any more. He's a *she*."

Charlie shrugged. "Since I don't know either of them, don't make much difference to me. What's the big deal."

This reaction wasn't at all what Keith was hoping for. He'd wanted to shock Charlie with the news of Alex's sex change, elicit a look of disbelief, pull him into a conversation about what a perv Alex must be to wear women's clothes.

Charlie smirked. "Is she cute?"

WORK AT THE DMV CONTINUED as always with no shortage of potential Pretty People to transform with his camera, but Keith found the thrill dissipating. He still snapped the unflattering shots but quickly deleted them. He felt fidgety and bored and couldn't find a way to make them fun again. He returned home after one particularly sluggish day, booted up his laptop, and found Alex's picture. He expanded it to full screen.

As Alex looked on, Keith rummaged through his closet to find the yearbook from their senior year. There was the old Alex. Like all the other boys, he wore a button up, his long bangs brushed smoothly across his forehead. Keith held the page up next to the screen. Good looking as either gender really. In the meantime, Alex's face had gotten softer, somehow, the gap between his front teeth now closed.

Keith read the inscription next to Alex's picture. Probably the same thing he'd written in all the other yearbooks that had circulated around their English classroom that warm day in June. "Brit Lit: It's been real. And it's been fun. But it hasn't been real fun! Good luck, A." Mr. Carson's literature class had been the last one they'd had together, and Keith remembered the teacher pointing out the line in the Wife of Bath's tale about her being gap-toothed. "Anyone in here have a space between their front teeth? Come on, everybody, smile."

"Alex, you have one. Know what that means?"

Alex shook his head.

"Means you're lusty!"

The class laughed, and Alex flexed his biceps. "Oh, yeah."

Mr. Carson opened his book. "Let's look at the Wife of Bath's tale and find all the signs of her lustiness."

Why did talk of Alex's lustiness bring heat to Keith's cheeks?

At his computer now, Keith realized he was getting firm and tried to figure out whether from the memory of Alex's lusty gap or the pretty picture of the new Alex or even the memory of fumbling around with Becca so many years ago.

Keith had picked a day when his mother worked late and Charlie had an appointment. He stopped at Becca's locker first thing in the morning. "Wanna come over after school?"

"I thought Charlie had to go to the ortho." In all the years they'd been playing video games together, he and Becca had played without Charlie only a handful of times.

"Yeah, but I feel like blowing off homework. My mom's working late, so we can turn it up, play without headphones."

When they got to the house, he settled her in the basement with a soda and some cookies and ran upstairs to brush his teeth, give his already-sweaty armpits a swipe of deodorant. At the top of the stairs, he paused, picturing the feel of her boobs in his hands. He could do this.

He plopped on the couch next to her. They never turned on the lights when they played, so the darkened basement felt like always. They played awhile, and, without thinking, he let her win—twice—before she finally said, "What's wrong with you? I never beat you twice in a row."

He set the game control on the coffee table and turned to face her. He'd rehearsed a big buildup about how they should be more than friends, that he'd been into her for a long time, and it was time to do something about it. But when he opened his mouth, the words disappeared. "Maybe I let you win, and now you owe me."

Her eyes got big. "You *let* me win? I don't think so. I kicked your ass." She picked up his controller and handed it to him. "Bring it."

She reset the game, and they started again.

He decided to toy with her awhile by running up his score, but then, as he was about to let her come back, he decided not to. He should beat her fair and square as usual. His thumbs went on autopilot while he tried again to think of his lines.

"Ha!" she yelled.

He refocused on the screen. What had happened?

She chugged the rest of her soda. "Tell me you *let* me win that one!"

He pictured her without the pudgy cheeks and zit on her forehead, imagined those thick lips on his—"I wanna kiss you." It had escaped against his will.

She froze. "Huh?"

He tried to think of something that would make his previous comment sound not so stupid, but he came up empty. "I want to kiss you." He leaned forward and looked into her eyes. What he saw there was a collage: disbelief, confusion, consideration, desire, disbelief again.

"Is this a joke?"

"No." He held up his hands. "No," he said again. "It's just," he decided to stay as close to the truth as possible and let the chips fall where they may. "I've been wondering what it would be like," he paused, "to kiss you." And then, to make sure she knew he wasn't messing with her, he said, "I thought it would be nice for my first kiss to be with," he hesitated again, "you."

The electronic hum of the TV filled the room while she considered his proposition and then, in true Becca style, said, "What the hell."

And they kissed. Tentatively, with awkward nose placement and breath holding and varying levels of pucker. He was trying to figure out what to do with his hands when he felt one of hers on his crotch, lightly at first, then more firmly. His eyes shot open. He was supposed to want this, right? Her tongue tried to part his lips, and he could think of nothing but a slug, a warm, persistent slug. She rubbed the front of his jeans harder but, no matter how much he tried, his dick just wouldn't respond.

What was wrong with him? "I can't—"

LIFE AT THE DMV CONTINUED in its slog. Lately, the road testers seemed to be tougher, so there were fewer photos to take than earlier in the month. To kill time, Keith opened a couple of old folders on his computer, deleted a few *Chimps*, tinkered around with a couple *Chumps*. He was about to empty the recycle bin when he looked up and saw Alex at one of the licensing stations. Again? Keith stood to make a dash for the break room to refill his coffee cup, but that would take him right into Alex's path. Better to keep his head down and play some solitaire until the coast was clear. He closed the incriminating tabs and clicked the button to deal himself a fresh hand.

It wasn't long before he realized he'd run out of moves, but he shuffled through the cards one more time looking for something he might have missed.

"Red seven on the black eight."

Keith jumped. "Jesus!" He fiddled with his mouse to close the window before his supervisor could bust him.

"Ohmygod. I'm so sorry!" It was Alex, eyes wide, a hand over her heart.

"Alex?"

"You remember my name? That's amazing. Anyway, I just stopped to thank you for my all-time best driver's license photo. I was in such a hurry when I was here before, I didn't look at it. But, thanks." Alex looked at Keith expectantly.

He knew he was supposed to say something but had no idea what.

Alex raised perfectly symmetrical eyebrows. "I guess you don't get too many people complimenting your work."

Still no idea what to say. Maybe if there was a question, he could answer it.

"Do you?"

There! "No, not really. People usually don't like their pictures. You'd be surprised how many of them don't complain though, no matter how bad their pictures are."

"I get that. I've had some terrible ones but never complained either." Alex slid the new license into a bedazzled wallet. "Well, anyway, thanks."

"You're welcome." Then it occurred to him. "If you didn't want a picture retake, why did you come back in today?"

"Oh, funny thing. Someone added 'senior' to my name, so technically I've been walking around with my father's license. Don't think he'd be too crazy to have a girl's face on his card." Alex's voice sounded light, but Keith could see sadness in those hazel eyes, too. "At least they can use the original picture you took."

Hopefully, they hadn't charged for the new license. "Good thing you got it all straightened out."

Alex laughed, "Straightened out! Yeah, in a sense, I guess," then squinted, took a breath as if to say something. Stopped.

Had Alex recognized Keith? Would the inevitable question come next: Do we know each other?

And would Keith tell the truth? Yeah, I might have had a crush on you in high school. I ruined a good friendship with a girl by using her to prove to myself I wasn't gay. I have successfully avoided any prospects of intimacy for my entire adult life because I don't know what the hell I'd do if I ever found myself attracted to someone else, man *or* woman.

"Well, thanks again, for the picture." And Alex was gone.

"Bye," Keith said too quietly for anyone to hear and watched Alex bounce away. That was the only way the movement could be described, "bouncing," and not in the affected, look-at-me bounce of the cheerleaders and Pretty Girls in high school but in the life-is-really-good bounce of a woman who had stopped giving a shit about what other people thought of her, who was good and truly happy. Keith didn't see *that* bounce very often, but he admired it when he did.

The waiting room was quiet. Keith opened his *Chimps* folder and took a couple notes on shots he planned to photoshop later, but his heart wasn't really in it. He was about to start in on the *Chumps* when his boss, Sandy, appeared over his shoulder. He x'ed out of the tab.

"Sandy. What's up?"

She didn't smile. "Come with me."

He took a deep breath, looked across the waiting area. A grim-faced road tester walked three steps ahead of a dejected-looking teenager. The girl would need no driver's license picture, but Keith held up his finger to Sandy. "In a sec." He pointed at the girl. "Might need a photo—"

"Now."

As he stood, Keith quickly cleared his search history.

Sandy crooked her finger at him. "Now."

With each step, Keith tried to convince himself he was being called in for something other than his photo collection. Maybe there had been too many requests for picture retakes. Maybe the asshole from last week who closed his eyes every damned time Keith clicked his mouse had complained.

Of course, Keith's hacks were the more likely reason. The one that allowed him to send photos from the DMV database to his personal email, the one that tacked a few extra hours onto his time sheet each pay period. Harmless stuff, really. And untraceable, he'd seen to it.

"Keith, sit down." She took a chair opposite him. He'd never seen a more uncomfortable face—and he'd seen a lot of those. "We need to address something that makes me very uneasy. We have been monitoring your computer for three months now."

His jaw tightened.

"And are quite disturbed—"

His armpits started to sweat.

"—by what we have noticed."

He remained perfectly still and concentrated on blinking: not too fast, not too slow. "Really?" He tried to add surprise to his voice without tipping into panic. "What did you notice?"

He didn't even try to look innocent, just focused on not looking guilty. There was a difference. Maybe he could cop to a lesser trespass and distract the higher-ups from something worse.

"We noticed numerous hours," here it comes, "on porn sites." She looked like she had eaten raw rhubarb. She slid a piece of paper across the desk. "This page lists the dates and duration of time spent looking at online pornography."

At first, Keith felt relief. Not only had Sandy *not* uncovered his hacks, but he hadn't actually performed the transgression of which he'd been accused. He was about to say as much when he realized someone *had* been watching all that porn and doing it using Keith's identity and login. If they could do that, what other access to Keith's identity did the guy have?

"I see you aren't going to try to deny it. That's the first step on the path to recovery." She handed him another piece of paper. "Nate won't let me fire you over this because it's your first offense in fifteen years, but you're suspended without pay for a month."

He looked at the paper without seeing it.

"When you return to work, your computer will be monitored. In the meantime, it will be scrubbed, and you won't be able to log in." And then, as if to prove she wasn't the inhuman monster so many of Keith's colleagues thought she was, Sandy handed him a sticky note with the phone number for a sex addiction hotline.

He nearly laughed out loud.

"This might be the wake-up call you need, Keith. Take advantage of it."

He adopted her tone. "Thank you, Sandy. I will."

KEITH'S FINGERS FOUND A RHYTHM. *Delete image?* Click. *Yes.* Click. *Delete image?* Click. Yes. Click. He didn't know why, but he felt the need to delete each one separately—maybe he was saying goodbye. The more pictures that flowed past his eyes, however, the more of a loser he started to feel like. What had made him save that one? Or that? Looking at them in bulk—like Sandy or whoever would scrub his work computer would see them—he could see his fixation as the mental imbalance it was. What had he been thinking? *Select all.* Click. *Delete.* Click. *Empty trash.* Click.

He knew they weren't completely gone, that little shadows of everything that had ever been on his machine remained, but it was a good bet no one would connect his home computer with the unflattering pictures he had taken at work. They would be looking for porn, after all.

And who the hell had been checking out porn using his work login? On the way out of the building with Jerry from HR a half-step behind him, Keith had scanned his coworkers for clues, but, as far as he could tell, they were busy with their end-of-day tasks and didn't think anything of the two men leaving the building together. No guilty looks. No sideways glances. Of course, his impersonator didn't need to be someone from this DMV. More likely, it was someone from somewhere else in the state. He could be all the way up in Superior or Green Bay. Keith was probably just an unlucky victim of a random hack.

Only one folder remained, the one with Alex's picture in it. Could he chance keeping it? Of course not. And why would he? There certainly wasn't any physical or sexual attraction there. Right? If anything, it was more a curiosity, a wondering if this new identity was real or some play for attention. But, the only people who would pay attention would be those who knew he had once been a guy. The picture on the screen looked like anything but. Seeing the hair and makeup and mannerisms, people would expect Alex to be a woman. People see what they expect to see.

Keith deleted the folder then double-checked that he'd emptied his trash, all he could do to cover his tracks. He shut down his computer and grabbed his keys. Might as well take advantage of being off work during the week and get his grocery shopping done while the store would be quiet.

As he pushed his empty cart through the produce section, he pondered how he could go about uncovering who had filched his identity. Maybe he could reverse engineer his own hacks. He absently picked up and put down cantaloupes, pulled a grape from a bunch and popped it into his mouth. Sour.

"You really shouldn't do that," the old lady next to him said, but kindly. "They haven't been washed."

"You're right." He put his conundrum behind him and moved on to the broccoli.

"The crowns are a better deal." Another woman with shopping advice, this time middle-aged with a toddler in her cart. "You don't pay for the stem that ends up in the compost anyway. Just sayin'."

"Thanks." He grabbed a head—a crown—at random and dropped it into a plastic bag.

He was about to steer his cart past the deli when he heard a familiar voice. "One pound of potato salad? Two?"

It was Alex. What the hell? Was the guy *every*where? He was consulting with an older lady riding a motorized scooter. The woman wore a bandana over what was obviously a bald head. A tube ran from her nose to a small machine in the basket in front of her.

Keith turned his cart to head down a different aisle. He didn't have it in him to deal with Alex's effervescence and endure an awkward introduction to the woman who he assumed to be Alex's mother. He'd skip the shaved ham.

Keeping an aisle between them, he finished his shopping and had made it through the check out and the first set of automatic doors when he almost smashed his cart into the back of Alex's mother's scooter. Keith stopped short, scanned the entryway for an escape route. No luck. Alex was at the front of the scooter grabbing the handlebars, full weight leaning backwards trying to pull the machine forward.

"Honey," the woman said, "let's just ask for help. Maybe the boy who bagged our groceries—"

"No, Ma," Alex struggled, high heels sliding on the tile floor. "I've got it."

But Alex didn't have it, not by a longshot, and Keith had nowhere to go but forward. He stepped around his cart. "Is there some way to put it into neutral so you can push it?"

"Oh my god! You're—" Alex pointed a blue-fingernailed hand, "the guy from the DMV. Ma, remember the photographer I told you about?"

Keith had used the word "photographer" on his job application form but had never heard anyone use the description for him and what he did at the DMV. Alex had told his mother about Keith?

The woman glanced over her shoulder, then at Alex expecting, Keith supposed, a name. Alex's eyebrows raised. "Yeah, uhm...?"

"Keith." The name was out before he could call it back. Now it was just a matter of time before the tumblers fell into place, and Alex's memory was jarred. Keith wondered if the hand on the ass would be part of the a-ha moment when Alex recognized him.

"I'm Margaret."

Keith took her hand. It was cold and dry. It felt like he could crush her bones. "Let me help you."

They found a way to get the scooter brake to let go, and Keith pushed from behind. The machine was heavier than he'd anticipated, and awkward, but they managed, inch-by-inch, to get it out the door.

"I can't believe we did it!" Alex beamed as if they'd summited a mountain. "Thank you so much!"

He could tell Alex thought the hardest part was over. "Need me to help get it to your vehicle?"

"That'd be gr—No wait, we walked, er I walked. She rode."

"It's my fault," said Margaret, "Alex wanted to drive, but it is such a lovely day."

Keith looked for an escape route. He'd done his good deed for the day. Now it was time to extract himself and let them solve their own problem. Alex was probably used to people stepping in to help. That's how the world treated Pretty People, especially those who looked like good-looking women who could use a protective hand. He knew he should try to offer them a lift or something. Maybe the scooter could fit in his trunk?

"'Scuse me?" The woman with the toddler was stuck behind Keith's cart.

He pushed it out of the way, apologized, thanked her again for the tip about the broccoli crowns. By the time he got to the curb, Alex was gone.

"Where did he—?"

"Alex dashed home for the van." Margaret reached for his hand. He let her take it. "Thank you for your help, Keith. We both appreciate it."

She let go. Her tone said goodbye, but he didn't feel right leaving her there alone. Maybe Alex's general flightiness made Keith want to make sure Margaret got into the van okay. How would Alex ever get the powerless scooter into the vehicle without help? Or maybe it was Keith's own mother's voice in his ear: *You left her there alone? Didn't I raise you better than that?*

"Why don't I keep you company until he gets back?"

"That would be nice. It's not far. *She*'ll be back soon." Margaret emphasized the *she*. "Nice of you to spend your day off looking after a sick old lady."

Day off? Of course. It was Wednesday, a normal day for a DMV employee to be at his post. He almost told her about his suspension but thought better of it.

Margaret made a visor with her hand and looked up at him. "I'm so glad *she* has a friend like you."

He flinched. "I—he—"

"Oh, I know you aren't *friends* exactly, but I'm grateful she knows at least one person who is willing to help her out in a pinch. Most of her friends from before moved away, and, well, let's just say people who stay in a place like this—" She stopped. "Well, they don't have the most open minds in the world. They wouldn't want anything to do with her, not now."

People who stay in a place like this. Keith had stayed in a place like this, and, of course, she was right: he normally wouldn't want anything to do with a cross-dresser or whatever Alex was. Still, he wanted to be bigger than Margaret's assessment of him and others like him. Who'd *stayed.*

"So many people get up on their high horses, thinking they're better than everyone else. They need that sense of power, I guess."

The Chimps and Chumps flashed across his brain. The truth of her words sank in his gut like a rock.

She sighed. "But not you. You don't care what's on the outside—even if you can't keep the pronouns straight."

She winked up at him.

What made her so certain of his goodness? "Oh, no, I—" He stopped himself. What was he going to say?

"It took me awhile to get them right, too. And at first, I didn't even try." She shook her head. Sighed. Pulled the tube from her nose to wipe it.

She replaced the cannula into her nostrils, smoothed the tube over each ear. "She quit her big, fancy job out in California to come back and help me. Bought the tricked-out van and this scooter. She didn't have to do any of that." She paused to catch her breath. "I probably won't make it to my next birthday, but this damned cancer gave me time with my child—with my daughter—I probably never would have—"

She coughed a long raspy cough, fished an inhaler out of her purse. It didn't help.

"Here, let me get you a bottle of water." He retrieved one from his cart, opened it, and handed it to her.

"Thank you so much." She took a big swallow, then a couple of long deep breaths. Her lungs wheezed. He was glad he'd stayed. "Tell your mother she raised you right."

His mother. How would she have reacted to anything in Keith's sexuality that turned out not to be middle lane? Not to mention his father. Keith could hear the derision in his voice. Their son's singlehood had probably always been a huge consternation for both of them. Most likely, they suspected he was gay, but if he showed up on their doorstep dressed like a girl? Forget it.

He told her about his mother, about how she brought him dinner every Thursday while his dad was at the gun club for the evening. She said she got lonely, but he could also tell that she appreciated being able to relax with him alone in a way she couldn't when his dad was around. She seemed to feel the need to keep them both in line when the three of them were together. "Keith, chew with your mouth closed." "Jack, don't hound him. The job he has is just fine." That kind of stuff.

Margaret tsked. "Fathers and sons. Such a tough relationship. My mother used to say, 'A son's a son until he takes a wife. A daughter's a daughter for all of her life.'" She chuckled. "But I say, 'A son's a son…until he's your daughter!'"

Keith caught a glimpse of the adoring mother she must have been gazing at a newborn Alex.

"Unfortunately, Alex's dad never wanted a daughter. Of course, I didn't believe in her new identity at first, either." She sighed, took another sip of water. "Sure, in retrospect, there were a few things that made sense—the drama, the experimenting with boys."

There it was then. The ass touch hadn't been his imagination.

KIM SUHR   •   69

"But there are plenty of actors who stay ac*tors* if you know what I mean," and then, in case Keith didn't get it, "not ac*tresses*."

She was laughing now.

"Seems like you have a beautiful relationship now."

Had he used the word, "beautiful?" He almost laughed. But of course, it was true. They did seem to have a beautiful relationship from the little of it he had seen.

Two quick beeps on a car horn interrupted his thoughts. Alex's arm waved madly from the minivan stopped at a red light.

"There she is." Margaret grasped Keith's hand. "Keith, promise me something." Her voice was urgent.

His throat clenched. Whatever she asked him to promise, he could tell it would make him squirm. He couldn't say "okay," but he couldn't say "no" either.

Her tug on his hand urged him into a squat, so he could look her in the eye. The fear he found there was palpable.

"It kills me to leave her—"

He started to object, pretend she'd be around for years to come.

"No. I know what's coming. I hate what I'm about to put her through." She wiped a tear. "She'll get over it, though, go back to her life in California eventually. In the meantime, I need to know there's one person *here* who will be good to her. One person *here* who doesn't see her as a freak. Please tell me that person will be you."

Her grip was desperate.

The van pulled in front of them. He stood.

"Keith?" Alex jumped out of the van, rounded the front of the vehicle. "Keith, oh my god, you stayed. You're the best."

The best? Definitely not. But maybe he could try.

BLANK

Isabelle turns the business card over and over.

Blank. APrayer4U.com. Blank. APrayer4U.com.

The business card is glossy, the words superimposed over a sepia photograph of praying hands.

Blank. APrayer4U.com. Blank. APrayer4U.com. Blank.

Like a sign flipper at the Liberty Tax place. Only there is no liberty for her in this stale hospital room so far from home. No liberty for her new husband staring ahead, his head hooked up to electrodes looking like one of those pictures of women getting a perm in the old days. His beautiful black hair has been shorn to optimize contact with the electrodes.

The door opens. The nurse, Ashley, walks in rubbing sanitizer into her hands. Her smile adds a glimmer of illumination to the dim room. "They told me you stayed overnight," she says to Isabelle. "I don't know how you do it."

The other nurses always go straight for the computer before talking to either Isabelle or Blake, but not Ashley. She takes hold of Blake's right foot, bends down so her eyes are level with his, raises her voice slightly. "How are you feeling today, Blake?"

Even though he has not answered this question—or any others since he came in—she waits as if a response is on its way. She grasps his feet and asks him to push against her hands. There is obviously no pushing on Blake's part, but

Ashley responds as if there was, "Great! Let's try that with your hands."

Isabelle doesn't know how much more of this she can take. The lack of clarity as to what is happening in Blake's brain, the doctors' inability to diagnose the problem. Will he be like this forever? Will she ever get to take him home? She starts to picture in-home healthcare nurses. A facility.

No. She can't go there yet. It has been only four days, five now that the sun has risen.

Blank. APrayer4U.com. Blank. APrayer4U.com. Blank.

Ashley finishes taking Blake's vitals, hanging his IV, emptying his urine bag. Isabelle can't imagine doing any of these tasks. That's why she got a job as far from taking care of people as possible. Computers. Logical machines that do only what you tell them to, nothing more. She doesn't have to put on a happy face to write code, no cheery small talk or holding someone's hand.

"Can I get you anything?" Ashley asks Isabelle. "I can order you some breakfast at least."

"Thanks." Isabelle forces a smile. "Maybe later."

"Okay." She holds her hands under the sanitizer dispenser again. "I'll be back. Let's get you better, Blake, so you can finish your honeymoon."

Out she goes.

BLANK. APRAYER4U.COM. Blank. APrayer4U.com. Blank.

Days later when it becomes clear that Isabelle has no intention of leaving the hospital until Blake does, Ashley brings in a package of underwear, another of socks. "You'll be amazed how much better you'll feel." She lets Isabelle use Blake's shower even though a sign says the bathroom is for patients only. "It's not like he'll be using it today anyway."

Ashley emphasizes the word "today," making it seem almost possible that he'll get up tomorrow and walk right into that shower.

Through all of this, Blake stares straight ahead. He blinks regularly. He sleeps. He doesn't respond one way or the other when the aides change his sheets. Was it really only a week ago they were drinking margaritas on the beach? Seven days since he strapped on the parasailing gear and floated up, up, up as the old Blake, the man she'd married, and returned to Earth inexplicably with none of his faculties intact.

Blank. APrayer4U.com. Blank. APrayer4U.com. Blank.

Prayers: Ha! Isabelle rejected the idea of God years ago when her minister-father first found out Blake was not a Christian—not an *anything* really. "An atheist." Her father spat the word as if it was a bitter root.

At the time, Isabelle didn't have the heart to confess that she had her own doubts about God and his healing powers. Sure, there was talk of a healer up near Fond du Lac who had cured a woman with early-onset Alzheimer's. What could explain such a thing besides God's intervention? Isabelle did agree that there was mystery. She just had a hard time attributing it to God.

The day her father dismissed Blake out of hand—Blake who was so good, good to her, good to his parents when they blamed themselves for their daughter's heroin overdose, good to the kids at the center where he volunteered—that was the day Isabelle gave up any notion of God once and for all.

Blank. APrayer4U.com. Blank. APrayer4U.com. Blank.

Where did the card come from? Did someone hand it to her in the ER waiting room? It doesn't matter. Maybe this is some kind of *sign*. She saw enough of them when she was a kid. Mrs. Albright coming into an inheritance just when the church needed a new boiler, for example. "A sign from God," her father said. "Praise be!"

Or the time that little Jackson Draper got his foot stuck in the train track with the Hiawatha bearing down on its way to Milwaukee. Isabelle was there, a huge panic rushing through her as his cloddy tennis shoe became lodged ever more solidly between the top of the track and the ground.

"God, help me!" Jackson screamed just before the horn blast drowned out his cries. The children joined Jackson's prayer at the top of their lungs, gave one last tug, and Jackson's foot slid out of the shoe. They all fell backwards in a heap.

It didn't occur to Isabelle until much later that night, as she tried in vain to fall asleep, that God could have just planted in one of their little brains to remove the shoe long before it became a life or death situation. Or, better yet, prevented the shoe from getting stuck at all. Maybe that was the moment the seeds of doubt had taken root.

Still, God *could* have been behind Jackson's rescue. She had no proof He wasn't, and that was the crux of the whole thing: it's pretty hard to prove that something *isn't* true.

Now here she sits with Blake, the only other person who has ever really understood her, who recognizes and respects her love of computer code, its elegance—divinity even. Blake knows how to reach across the chasm that separates her from others. He knows *her*.

Or rather, he *knew*.

What can he know now, nearly as lifeless as Jackson's empty shoe? She pulls a hand across her cheek and kisses his forehead. "I'll be right back."

Down the hall, she finds the family waiting room and slides into a chair, turns on her phone. Text after text pops up, and, from their tone, she realizes she has neglected to convey the severity of Blake's condition. Her mother-in-law: "Hoping Blake has turned the corner and you're back on the beach!" Her sister, Angel: "Speedy recovery to Blake!" The neighbor: "Don't worry about a thing. I'll take care of Kipper. You just get Blake better and get home safe!"

Maybe she has minimized the situation to avoid people's "thoughts and prayers." Ever since she parted ways with her father, she has balked at the idea of people interceding with God on her behalf—at times, telling them so in no uncertain terms.

But what of this? Blank. APrayer4U.com. Blank. APrayer4U.com.

Perhaps, the card has come into her hands for a reason. Maybe God has put Blake into this mysterious condition to bring her back to Him. Stories like this abounded in her father's sermons. It wouldn't be the first time He had tested one of His children. Right?

Once she has opened that door, the language returns easily to mind. *Seek and ye shall find. Knock and the door shall open. Ask and it shall be given.*

What does she have to lose really?

She takes a deep breath and prepares to turn back her years of disbelief. She'll go to the website on the card and put in a request for the prayer chain. An intercession on Blake's behalf. When he is better, she'll convince him of God's healing power. She readies herself to make amends with her father. Anything to get Blake back.

She opens the browser on her phone and types *APrayer4U.com.*

Internet service here is ridiculously slow. She watches the palm trees sway outside the window and imagines this nightmare over, re-starting her honeymoon with her husband—her husband!—Thanks be to God!

The search is nearly over.

Her screen blinks once, twice. She checks the charge on the battery. Twelve percent. The blinking stops. She can taste the margarita, feel the warm sea air on her face, Blake's warm breath on her neck.

A mostly white screen stares back at her. Where she expected to see a graphic of praying hands or a button for a prayer request, she finds florescent green text and a cartoon drawing of an astronaut: "Oops! It seems aliens have stolen content from this page. But you can create your own website and fill it with the best content on Earth!"

Isabelle powers down her phone, tosses the card in the trash, and heads back to Blake's room.

PLAY-SCHOOL

Willie sits at the top landing of the basement stairs, a small pile of paint peelings next to his thigh. He wedges his thumbnail under a nice long ribbon where the wood has rotted underneath and pulls off another satisfying strip. In the playroom below, his sister, Mary teaches a math lesson to her friends, Abby and Grace. Her tone alternates between their mother's mildly annoyed voice and the sing-songy rhythm of every teacher at their school. Right now, she's mildly annoyed. If Willie were in the game, she wouldn't be so crabby because, despite being in first grade, he already knows his addition and subtraction facts. She wouldn't have to repeat herself so many times.

If only he weren't in a Time Out. He can't even remember what he did to receive the punishment and has been up here so long he wonders if Mary forgot to set the timer. His thumb finds another blister in the paint and starts working on it.

Three months ago, his mother had warned his dad to take care of the rot before painting the steps, but instead, Dad gave the stair a few quick swipes with sandpaper and sucked up the dust with a shop-vac. Willie had wanted desperately to be the one pulling the paintbrush across the step, the one in charge for a change. But his only job that day was to hold the ashtray for his dad and stay one step behind him as he painted his way down the stairs. Now, Willie feels a puff of pleasure with every sliver he peels away, undoing his father's work. He starts to separate them into groups like Mary taught him to practice counting by fives.

"Teachers!" Mary has deepened her voice to sound like the principal's over the intercom.

Shoot! He's going to miss it. He knows what she will say next before she makes the announcement: "It is time to begin our lockdown drill. Please lead your students through the proper procedure."

"Okay, children." Her tone has changed back into teacher mode. "You need to be very quiet."

She has gotten better at giving her voice a combination of alarm—to let the kids know she means business—and calm assurance—so the kids don't go crazy and start screaming. That could mean death to them all.

"Miss Buck?" Abby's half-whisper is barely audible. "I want my mom."

This is usually Willie's line.

"Shhhhh." She instructs the girls to crouch down and make themselves as small as possible. "And no one is allowed to use the bathroom."

This line is new, but Willie knows where it came from. There was an active shooter drill on Wednesday, and their mother had to be called to pick them both up before the school day ended. As they walked to the car, he noticed Mary was wearing a pair of pink stretchy pants he didn't recognize—probably borrowed from the health room—and she carried a plastic Pick 'n Save bag with what looked like her favorite green pants and maybe a pair of undies inside.

"But I have to go!" Grace's voice sounds desperate.

Now that it has come up, Willie feels the urge to go to the bathroom, too.

"You'll have to hold it, and, if you can't, just pee your pants. That's okay. You won't get in trouble."

And Mary didn't get into trouble. In fact, their mom stopped for dishes of frozen custard, something she never did, and allowed them to eat in the car on the way home. Willie polished off his before they got to their subdivision, but Mary's dish—melted and refrozen—is still in the freezer waiting for her to "get her appetite back" as their mother put it.

Willie considers abandoning the step to help himself to his sister's abandoned treat. That would teach her to put him in Time Out and forget about him.

"Okay, children. I'm going to turn off the lights now. You need to be quiet like little mice."

The basement goes dark. Willie is grateful for the light coming from the kitchen above. Now is the time in the game where the children try to stay completely silent while an imaginary man with a gun tries to find them in their darkened classroom. If Mary can count to 100 without anyone saying anything, they win and their lives are saved. If not, well…

Mary always counts in her head, and the time it takes is impossibly long. They have survived only three times so far. Their deaths have been Willie's fault every time. Maybe that's why Mary has put him in Time Out to begin with: to give the class a fighting chance. Still, he wants to take part. He has grown to enjoy the rush that moves through him as they wait to see if they will survive another day—and the pride on Mary's face when they do.

Wait. The Nerf blaster he got for Christmas! It's fully automatic and holds fifty rounds. He pictures himself armed and bounding down the steps. This time someone else will be the one to give them away. She can't put them all in Time Out, can she?

Willie stands as quietly as he can and walks up the three remaining steps to the kitchen. As he passes his parents' bedroom doorway, he remembers the Nerf gun is still in the basement where he left it. Shoot, again!

Maybe he has another weapon in his room. He could pretend his light saber is a gun. Maybe the sword from his knight costume in the dress-up bin. Then he gets a better idea. The nightstand on his dad's side of the bed: there is a gun in there. A real one. A pistol. Once, Willie used the key on the hook hanging on the back of the nightstand to open the locked drawer, just to look at it. He listens for the lawn mower. Dad's still out there. Mom won't be home for hours. He could just—

Thump! Thump! Thump!

He jumps. What's that? He scrambles back toward his perch. Mary can't possibly have made it to 100 already.

THUMP! THUMP! THUMP!

His heart starts to race, and he feels a surge move through his body.

"Oh no, children. That means he's getting closer. You need to be extra quiet."

THU—

"SSSSTTTTTTOPPP!" Abby's scream makes his ears hurt. And Mary does stop. He can hear nothing but the ticking of the clock in the kitchen.

Then one of them starts to cry. The sound reminds him of Maesie's kittens right after they were born. Their eyes were tiny slits, and he asked his mom if Maesie had given birth to a whole litter of blind cats. "All kittens are born with their eyes closed," his mother explained. "They open after a few days and then can see as clearly as you or me."

He wishes whoever is crying would stop. It sounds like Grace.

The light goes on.

"Now, children," Mary's voice is gentler than before. "This is only a drill. Everyone is okay. See? Look! No one else is here. That pounding was just me. See?"

More thumps, not as loud this time.

"But…we're…dead…" Grace can barely get the words out.

"No, see? We're alive. We just have to practice this, so we can save our own lives if it ever comes to that."

Her voice sounds like their mother's did on the way home from school. Willie tries to remember if Mary was crying then, but all he can recall is wondering why she was letting her frozen custard melt. Wasn't she going to eat that?

"Now," her voice is back-to-business, "we need to evacuate the building. Where is my emergency backpack?"

Willie knows she won't find the red-string backpack stocked with a makeshift first-aid kit, a class list with names and phone numbers of made-up students, an old cell phone, and a pack of bubble gum. When they get to the oak tree on the corner, their designated meeting spot, Mary likes to say, "Good job, children. Today you saved your own lives," and give each of her students a piece of Bubblicious. But today, she won't have any gum to give them because Willie chewed what remained after their last game of play-school. He tried to hide the backpack under a box at the foot of the stairs, but he sees it peeking out plain as day. It's just a matter of time before Mary discovers it.

Abby finds her voice. "Miss Buck, we don't have time to grab ANYthing! We just need to GO!" Her voice gets louder as she talks. She must be moving toward the steps. Soon, they'll all be heading up for the evacuation. Mary will find the pilfered backpack with its missing gum. Then, he'll be in real trouble, maybe banished from the game forever.

It's too late to go back for the pistol. Maybe another time. Instead, he grabs one of his dad's work boots. When he clicks off the basement light, it's as if the switch is connected to a scream machine. Mary's is the loudest of all.

He bangs the boot on the top step, scattering the paint peelings and relishing the blast of power he feels. And, even though he knows he shouldn't, he makes his voice as scary as he can. "Here I come!"

RINK RAT

Most people will tell you cold doesn't have a smell, but it does. In an ice rink, the smell of cold blends with that of sweaty leather, Zamboni exhaust, and hot dogs steamed in a Nesco all day. This is the smell of hockey. It is a smell that will forever remind me of my eleventh year. It will forever remind me of Arnie. The Year of Arnie was the year I learned about winning. And about losing.

Oh, I knew plenty about losing hockey games. "Shell shocked" is what my dad called it. Even in Ice Mice, where we didn't keep score, it didn't take Einstein to recognize that the other team put the puck in the net a lot more—a *lot* more—than our team did. I'd overhear parents chuckling that the ice sheet started to slant downhill towards our goal because we spent so much time on that side of the rink defending it. I believed this as truth and figured that the tilting ice was why we switched goals halfway through our hour of ice time: to even it out.

Our losing trend continued through Squirts. It would have followed me into Pee Wees, too, but in 1978, the Hockey Association changed the birthday cut-off date to move to the next level. That year, I went from being the oldest Squirt to being the youngest Pee Wee. The change meant leaving most of the players I'd grown up with. It also meant being on a winning team for the first time in my young hockey career.

By mid-January, we found ourselves with a 12–2 record, and parents started to talk to each other in hushed tones about The State Tournament. I could hear the capital letters in their voices. "Should we make hotel reservations now, just in case we make it to State?"

"We don't want to jinx ourselves."

"But rooms go fast in Stevens Point. We don't want to have to drive all the way from Wausau."

"Yeah, and Dean and other boys will want a pool."

It was about this time I started to stay after practice to work on my backhand with my dad, our assistant coach. While the other kids were loosening their skates and packing their duffel bags, Dad would feed me pass after pass as I raced toward an open net trying to catch the puck on the back of my stick, dribble, and lift it into the corner. With an open net, this should have been easy, but not for me. Puck after puck went wide. Some just plain stopped in the crease. Quite a few sailed past my stick through my feet. I was relieved we were alone for these drills. Pete, the rink manager, was busy in other parts of the building getting ready to close up: turning off lights in the locker room, unplugging the Nesco, emptying the popcorn machine. He gave us fifteen—sometimes thirty—minutes before he climbed up on the Zamboni one last time for the day.

One night following a particularly humiliating series of passes and misses, a miracle happened. First, I caught the puck on the sweet spot of my stick. Then, like a force guided my hands in just the right pattern, I straightened my right arm, twisted my torso, and lifted the puck into the corner of the net. Instinctively, I raised both arms in victory. As Dad skated toward me offering a high-five, I heard a cheer from the bleachers.

"Way to go, Deano!" It was muffled but unmistakable.

I looked up into the stands, and there stood Arnie, wearing his striped knit hat with the pom-pom as big as a grapefruit dancing on top. He was shaking his fist in the air and jumping up and down on the aluminum bleachers. Embarrassed and proud at the same time, I cranked my arm in his direction.

"I didn't know Arnie was watching us," I said in the dark car on the way home.

"He stays every Thursday. You've never noticed him before?"

"*Every* Thursday?" I thought of all the missed passes and all the missed shots. My face flushed. "I thought we were alone."

"Ah, Arnie's a rink rat. He's always around. Pete says most days Arnie's there when he opens up. Sometimes he doesn't leave until the last light is turned off. He even used to help with the goals at the end of the night, but he can't do that anymore."

"Why not?"

"One night, he was daydreaming, and Pete nearly ran him over with the Zamboni."

ONCE I STARTED PAYING ATTENTION, I noticed Arnie everywhere: razzing the opposing team's goalie from behind the glass, doing a victory dance after we won in overtime. Although he watched team after team, day after day, he showed loyalty to us even when we played one of our own in-town rivals whose practices he also attended, whose players he also knew. We were starting to see him as our mascot.

"Hey, Arnie, tell us about when *you* went to State," Billy Johnson yelled throwing a tape ball that missed Arnie's head by inches.

"Yeah, tell us."

"Yeah!"

Arnie's eyes twinkled with the attention. "When I was a boy," his voice was like walking down a hill, "just like you," he leaned forward a little bit, "it was The State Tournament. The score was tied. The other team pulled their goalie." He paused. Now his voice started walking uphill. "I had an open net for a backhand shot. A backhand, ya know?" He looked straight into my eyes until I looked away. "And I missed. I missed! Boy, was my dad mad at me!"

"So, what did he do, Arnie?" yelled Tim Hanson in a voice that sounded like he already knew the answer. He was egging Arnie on, but I didn't know why.

"On the way home, he was yelling at me. He tried to give me a smack and put the car in the ditch!" He punctuated his point by plucking off his hat, "A hundred fifty-seven stitches!"

"Ahhhhhh!" the boys yelled.

He tipped his head so we could get a good look. His eyes twinkled at the reaction.

Mouth open, I stared at the misshapen skull, the stubbly crew cut with a bald patch where the stitches must have been. I don't know if I was more shocked by the gruesomeness of his head or the facts of his story. Arnie had been normal once, just like me. He'd gone to State, and now he was—what? My mom said he was "limited" when she talked about Arnie. Dad said he was "slow." The boys on the team called him a "retard" when he wasn't around.

"Now you boys, work on your backhands, so your dad don't put the car in the ditch on the way home." He shook his finger at us. My teammates laughed and repeated his words with the same inflection.

Arnie put his hat back on and headed to the bleachers. The other guys picked up where they'd left off with their post-game banter. Jeff Martin gave Tim Swenson a noogie. Paul Phillips pulled his cup out of his jock, held it over Andy Johanssen's face. "Oxygen. He needs oxygen!" while Andy struggled to free himself.

Our captain, Sam Fitzgibbon, elbowed me, "How do ya like that? Go all the way to State and miss an open net goal," Fitz shook his head. He was the oldest and biggest on the team. I idolized him.

Once our belts were fastened and the defroster began to clear the windshield, I asked, "Dad, Arnie's car accident, you know, is that what made him slow?"

"Yeah, he was quite a hockey player, a pretty sharp kid, too. Unfortunately, he had a dad with a terrible temper."

"Did his dad hit him a lot?" The only time I could remember my own dad hitting me was when I'd run in front of Grandpa's tractor, and, even then, he'd apologized afterward.

"Yeah. But the accident ended that." He paused. "His old man didn't make it."

WITH OUR FINAL WIN of the regular season, our team was 23–5. The next weekend was regionals, and we found ourselves seeded against the West Side Warriors, the team with the worst record in the league. We had already beaten them twice, but what should have been an easy win turned out to be two periods of humiliation. We were scoreless to their three goals, and some of our players spent more time in the penalty box than on the ice. As the first line players tried to catch their breath and Coach tried to light a fire under us between periods, Arnie jumped down into the players' box.

"C'mon, boys. You can do it!" He shook his fist at us like the coach was doing. Surprised to see Arnie in the box, we stopped listening to Coach. Then Arnie started chanting, "All the way to State!" He chanted with increasing volume, so it wasn't just us guys in the box who could hear him. The other team looked over at our bench. Arnie was yelling the words reserved for teams that were winning by a huge margin, who really *were* about to go to State. As things were, we weren't going anywhere but home with our tails between our legs. Arnie had broken a hockey taboo almost as bad as uttering the words "shut out" before the final buzzer.

But despite our embarrassment at a "limited" man in a rainbow-striped stocking cap chanting all by himself—or maybe because of it—we joined in. The coach gave up his speech and shouted the chant, clapping as he yelled, "All the way to State! All the way to State!"

The buzzer signaled the end of the break. Our first line skated out to their positions for the face off. Luke won it and passed the puck to Andy who dribbled toward the opposing goal, skated around the net and stuffed it in the corner. Our bench erupted. Parents jumped out of their seats and gave high-fives. Arnie banged the plexiglass.

It took three more shifts for the next goal, a slapshot off Andy's stick, to sail neatly over their goalie's right shoulder. This time, Arnie got the parents chanting. He flapped his arms bringing them to their feet.

Seven long minutes passed on the clock without a goal for either side. Coach called a time out. The parents sat down. Our bench quieted to get instructions. Through their masks, my teammates looked grave. Three minutes, thirty-two seconds and two goals stood between us and Sectionals. We could very possibly lose to the worst team in the league.

"You okay, Billy?" asked Coach as Billy took a big puff off his inhaler, held the breath in his lungs. He nodded and started coughing. He hung his head between his knees.

"Alternate shifts with Dean. I don't want you falling over out there. The rest of you, pass, pass, pass just like we do in practice. They're getting tired. Work for the clean shot. No junk."

My heart raced. Alternating with Billy meant I would be playing every other shift with Tim and Sam as my forwards. Those guys passed the puck right to your stick. They caught passes that would fly past other players. They picked up their own rebounds. I was used to playing on lines with the other mediocre players on the team. Now I would be skating with the guys who had scored nearly all the goals of the season. Since I couldn't bite my nails through my gloves and mask, I tapped my stick on the bench until it was my turn to go out there.

"Go get 'em, Deano!" I heard Arnie call.

It was one of those fluke things, one of those plays you dream about where the player for the opposing team totally misses the puck and it lands right on the blade of your stick. You dribble left, right, left again toward the goal. You straighten your right arm and twist your torso to give the shot even more power. You push off your left skate and let it go and watch while the goalie lifts his glove a split second too late and the puck wobbles right over his shoulder. Your teammates are hitting your helmet and giving you high-fives and hitting you on the butt with their sticks. And the parents are on their feet yelling, "All the way to State! All the way to State!" And Arnie is throwing his hat in the air and not catching it and having to crawl under the bleachers to retrieve it. And Coach is saying, "Atta boy, Deano!" and, after Andy completes his hat trick, you feel a part of the final victory as you never have before.

ARNIE BECAME NOT ONLY OUR mascot but our good luck charm as well. Before the sectional game against Portage, he stood at the door to the rink and each of us touched his pom pom before putting our first skate on the ice. He whacked our behinds and gave us each an order, "Go get 'em!" "Kick butt!" "Fire up!" "Kill 'em!" Over his threadbare dress shirt, he wore the Southside Saints jersey onto which one of the moms had stitched "Rink Rat" where his name would normally go. He was number 99. Coach said Arnie could stand in the players' box and help out by opening the door for shift changes. He wasn't as quick on the door as Coach was, but he never left anyone standing on the ice waiting to get in or vice versa.

And so it was after the victory over Portage that Arnie was on the team bus on our way to Stevens Point for The State Tournament. Since my mom was on call that weekend and couldn't get anyone to cover for her, I would share a bed with Dad, and Arnie could have our extra bed at the Holidome.

The morning of our first game, Dad shook me awake. He and Arnie were already dressed. Dad held a steaming styrofoam cup of coffee. Arnie was downing the last of his can of Hawaiian Punch.

"It's show time, Deano." Arnie smiled, pulled on his hat, and left the room.

The State Tournament provided just enough ceremony to make us feel like celebrities. A banner with each team's logo hung over the ice sheet. Instead of names of just the first line players being announced, every member of every team was introduced before each team's first game of the tournament. The players skated out one by one until they stood shoulder to shoulder on the blue line facing the flag. Nervous about my own introduction, I debated whether I should high-five only the last guy announced or if I should go through the whole line of guys tapping each one on the butt with my stick as the other guys did. Weighing the pros and cons of each, I missed the announcement of my name. Fitz's glove to the back of my helmet snapped me alert.

"Deano, that's you!" sang Arnie from the bench.

I nearly tripped on my way out of the box but righted myself before my second skate hit the ice. A single high-five to Tim was all I dared.

With the excitement of the pregame ceremonies over, it took only one shot and one save for this to feel like any other hockey game. We skated handily toward our first win in the single-game elimination tournament. The other goalie had over thirty saves, but we still won, 4 to 1.

In our second game, the Superior team didn't buckle quite so easily, but by the final buzzer we were up by a goal. We took to the stands to find out which team we would play for the championship.

By Sunday morning, we had played and watched enough of the tournament to pick up the moves of the other teams. None of us had ever seen a player lift his knee and glide around on one skate making a cranking motion with his opposite arm after scoring a goal. It must have been something they did Up North. The move became the victory dance of anyone on our team who scored a goal.

Arnie, too, was picking up on the other fans' gestures. Using their arms and legs, fans for the Ashwaubenon team started spelling words for the fans to chant. "Give me an A! Give me an S!" It took quite a while to spell Ashwaubenon. This gave Arnie plenty of time to study their moves. Even though the *i* came before the *a* in Saints most of the time when he spelled it, he did a nice job of firing up our fans in between periods. Our fans just spelled "S-A-I-N-T-S" regardless of what letters Arnie's contortions looked like.

We would play Eau Claire for the championship. Talk around the rink was that they would be seriously out of their element when they faced us. By fluke, they had played the weakest teams through the early rounds and had lost their starting goaltender to a groin injury. Coach warned us that they would try to draw us into penalties and that we should keep our heads cool and our sticks down. Their strategy backfired, and they spent a lot of time playing short-handed themselves. By the time we were up by five goals, Coach was rotating all four lines evenly, and I was seeing lots more ice than I had all year.

My second goal of the season came in a five-on-three situation. I intercepted a pass and had a breakaway. As I crossed the blue line, I lost my footing and almost lost the puck, but somehow, I caught my balance and continued toward the goal. I deeked left and shot for the lower right corner. As I got back to the bench, Dad gave me a high-five and a swat on the butt. Expecting Arnie's "Way to go, Deano!" I was a little disappointed when I looked at his usual spot and he wasn't there.

Then I heard his voice.

"Give me a D!"

I'm sure he put two *e*'s in my name, but the crowd spelled it right. Goosebumps rose under my pads as I heard my name chanted by what seemed like a thousand people.

A few more minutes and we were Pee Wee Champs. Eau Claire's captain was accepting the second-place trophy, and we were lining up along the boards to have our names called to receive our medals. This time, I skated out on cue. I even remembered to remove my glove before offering my right hand to the league commissioner. Finally, our captain and coaches were invited to center ice to accept the trophy. As Fitz skated and the coaches walked on the red carpet rolled out for this purpose, we noticed Arnie standing alone in the players' box.

"Arnie! Arnie!" someone started chanting. We all joined in.

Soon, Dad was walking back to the bench, putting an arm around Arnie and urging him to join us. Arnie shook his head and pushed Dad away lightly. Finally, he gave in. He took off his hat, curled it up in one fist, and ran his other hand over his hair. He stood up straighter and seemed to walk with less of a limp as he got closer to the award. Fitz, Coach, Dad and Arnie held up the trophy, which was hardly big enough to warrant two hands much less the four that held it.

"I THINK FITZ SHOULD KEEP IT. He's the captain," Billy yelled from the back of the bus.

"What about making it a traveling trophy? Ya know, everyone could keep it for a couple weeks and then give it to the next guy."

Coach whistled, and we all quieted down. "Guys, when I said I thought someone else should keep the trophy, I had someone *else* in mind."

He nodded at Arnie stretched across the back seat of the bus. Impossibly, he had fallen asleep before the bus had pulled out of the parking lot. Even Coach's whistle hadn't awakened him.

"Next month, he's going to move to Florida, so his sister can take care of him. His mom just can't do it anymore." He paused to let it sink in. "This is his last shot at getting a State trophy." The bus grew silent. "Whaddya think?"

I was the first to raise my hand with a thumbs-up. A unanimous vote decided it.

A WEEK LATER AT THE BANQUET, Coach presented Arnie with the trophy and a green and white Saints baseball cap.

"It's a little warm in Florida for a stocking cap," he joked as he placed the hat on Arnie's head. He gave the bill a wiggle and a flick. "We'll miss ya around the rink, Arnie."

Soon, we were on our feet chanting, "Arnie! Arnie!"

His face turned redder as the volume increased. Fitz headed for the front of the room. We followed. We gave Arnie high-fives and pats on the back. He gave us noogies and started the wave. Soon, a roomful of dressed up hockey players and their parents were reaching for the ceiling singing, "ooooOOOOO," as the wave circled the room. The wave slowed, and my eyes met Arnie's. As he walked toward me, I hoped that he wouldn't start to spell my name with his limbs. Something that was cool in an ice rink would be just plain embarrassing at a banquet. Instead, he pulled his stocking cap onto my head and put his arm around my neck. "I'll miss ya, Deano. Keep working on that backhand."

TWENTY-FIVE YEARS LATER, I lace my skates and pull on my gloves. Even though most of the concessions come from vending machines now, the rink still smells like it did when I was a kid. Sometimes, I even expect to see Arnie up in the stands misspelling my name or stomping on the aluminum seats. I dig around in my bag for my whistle, and a flash of stripes catches my eye. Tonight, I'll stay after practice and shoot backhands at my daughter, so she can work on her skate saves. Maybe tonight I'll tell her about Arnie.

THE DIP

BETWEEN US AND OUR FRIEND

6.7.22 *ping*

From Jacki
To Maura & Kristal

You guys, check your email.

From Maura
To Jacki & Kristal

No Lynette?
What's up?

From Jacki
To Maura & Kristal

No biggie. Just read your email.

* * *

FROM: Jacqueline Sorenson <jsoren@cjc.edu>
TO: Maura McElroy <mcelroy.m@cyrc.org>
Kristal Moore <kmooreorless63@gmail.com>
DATE: June 7, 2022
SUBJECT: Let's do this!

Hi guys,

How's it going? It's been too long since we've seen each
other, and I feel bad about how we left things on our last
trip to Lynette and Trent's cabin—totally my fault, I know.

Anyway, I got out of teaching summer classes, and, with James gone (good riddance!), I'll have plenty of time on my hands this summer. Too much!

How 'bout I make nice w/Lynette and get her to invite us Up North for old times' sake? Maybe just a long weekend instead of a full week. (I'm not crazy!) Third weekend in August like always.

Please say yes. I miss you guys!

Smooches,

Jacki

* * *

From: Kristal Moore <kmooreorless63@gmail.com>
To: Maura McElroy <mcelroy.m@cyrc.org>
    Jacqueline Sorenson <jsoren@cjc.edu>
Date: June 7, 2022
Subject: RE: Let's do this!

Hey Y'all,

It's SO good to hear from you, Jacki. I miss you and Maur. *<deleted: While>* The thought of heading North is tempting, *<deleted: a weekend of Lynette and her Trump-etting and our having to listen because it's her place....>* surrounded down here, as I am, by so much MAGA *<deleted: bullshit>* nonsense (I know, "nonsense" isn't really my style, but I'm trying to replace swear words in my vocabulary. Janna would kill me if my granddaughter's first word is "bullshit." :)), time with you two would be more than a relief.

From the way things went down last summer, though, I'm not sure I'd be excited about being with Lynette again. I imagine that her parroting of the "Gospel According to

Trump and Trent" *<deleted: remind me why she married him!?!?>* has only gotten worse since then. *<deleted: Plus, I'm sure she hasn't been vaxxed, which, I'm sorry, is just plain selfish. She obviously doesn't...>*

Maybe just the three of us could meet up somewhere else. I hear there's always something going on in Chi-town. (Hint. Hint, Maura!)

Hugs,

Kristal

* * *

From: Maura McElroy <mcelroy.m@cyrc.org>
To: Jacqueline Sorenson jsoren@cjc.edu
Kristal Moore <kmooreorless63@gmail.com>
Date: June 8, 2022
Subject: RE: Let's do this!

Hi, You Two,

I love the idea of getting the "band" back together—*all* of us. Much as I agree it'll be hard to be with Lynette again, I think it's a good idea to try. Somehow, we need to start building bridges back to each other, and, if we leave her out, that'll make Trent and his MAGA cronies look all that much more appealing to her. Maybe if we keep reminding her of our shared background together, reminisce, make some fun new memories—pull her in closer instead of pushing her away—she may even open up just a little bit.

That's my two cents. Thanks for thinking of it, Jacki. It's on my calendar.

Good luck with Lynette!

Maura

FROM: Jacqueline Sorenson <jsoren@cjc.edu>
To: Maura McElroy <mcelroy.m@cyrc.org>
        Kristal Moore <kmooreorless63@gmail.com>
Date: June 8, 2022
Subject: RE: RE: RE: Let's do this!

You guys always did overthink stuff. I just wanted a weekend of drinking with my old pals and another chance to take The Dip in Crystal Lake. And you got all political on me. Lynnie is ON BOARD! I called her right after I sent you the email. I probably should have told you that *before* you went to the trouble of answering. (Your thoughts *were* very deep, though. ;-P) Say what you want about her, the girl doesn't hold a grudge.

I figured I'd go whether you guys wanted to or not. Now you'll just look like heels if you blow it off. No pressure (Kristal—cough! cough!). Ha!

Let's do potluck. I shared a Googledoc. Fill in what you want to bring. The wine's on me. I joined a wine club during covid and am slowly drinking through the cases they delivered right to my doorstep. (Silver linings!) Let's leave Lynnie out of the food/drink responsibilities since she's putting us up—unless you think *not* including her will drive her into the arms of the MAGA camp!

See you in August!

Ta!

Jacki

* * *

Google Doc shared by Jacki Sorenson

Message: Hey, Bitches, Please put your name next to the things you want to bring to share. I'm taking care of the wine/whine: Is it 5:00 yet??!?!? It's 5:00 somewhere!

Everybody: bring a salty snack (or 2) and something chocolate (or 2 or 4) to share.

We'll be together soon!

Thurs

Dinner

Soup (Maura: Veggie chili)
Salad/Dressing (Maura)
Bread/Butter (Jacki)

Fri & Sat

Self-serve breakfast stuff (bagels, cream cheese, yogurt, granola, etc): _____
Coffee (Jacki)
HALF&HALF! (Jacki) (Maura, bring your own oat milk or whatever)

Lunch
Sandwich stuff (Maura—and, yes, Jacki, I'll bring some meat. There's a great locally-sourced deli nearby. Just because I don't eat meat doesn't mean I want to control your diet. I'll leave that to karma :))
CHIPS! _____
Mayonnaise-y deli salad _____
Fruit (Jacki)

Fri Dinner
Stuff for the grill (Jacki: steak & corn.) (Maura: Boca burgers. I'll share with the rest of you! :))
CHIPS! (Maura)
Green Salad_____

Sat Dinner (Let's go to Walt's Supper Club—brandy old-fashioneds on Jacki!)

Sun

Breakfast
Leftovers (Maura: I'll stop in Racine and pick up Kringles on my way.)

* * *

From: Kristal Moore <kmooreorless63@gmail.com>
To: Jacqueline Sorenson jsoren@cjc.edu
Maura McElroy <mcelroy.m@cyrc.org>
Lynette Thompson <l.thompson11.6@hotmail.com>
Date: July 1, 2022
Subject: Can't make it

Hi Y'all,

<deleted: After giving this a lot of thought, I have decided I can't join you for the weekend in August. Tabitha is just too vulnerable and knowingly being in the same airspace with someone who has chosen not to get vaccinated or boosted—and, Lynette, your reposts on social media about vaccines make it abundantly clear that you don't care about protecting yourself and others from covid—seems like I would just be asking for it. Cystic fibrosis is no joke. How could I ever explain to Janna infecting her only child? How could I ever live with myself? I miss the days when we could be together in a carefree way, laughing and...>

I'm so sorry, but I'm not going to be able to make it up to the cabin this time. Thank you for the invitation, Lynette. I hope you all enjoy.

Hugs,

Kristal

_____

7.2.22 *ping*

From Maura
To Kristal

Hey, got a min for a call?

> From Kristal
> To Maura
>
> Tabby just fell asleep in my lap
> and has a death grip on my earlobe.
> Can't talk, but can text.

From Maura
To Kristal

Okay. Just saw your email. I'm
sad you won't be at Lynette's.
Everything okay?

> From Kristal
> To Maura
>
> Yeah, I'm sure L isn't vaxxed. Can't risk bringing
> covid back to Tabby—or getting
> it myself. I'm it for childcare.
> Don't want to leave
> Janna in the lurch.
>
> ...

...

And TBH I'm pissed at
L's hypocrisy.
*<deleted:Remember
her rant about the Hasidic Jews
not vaxxing and the measles outbreak?
All judgy about them but now
no qualms about infecting MY grandbaby.
I guess I'm starting to take this stuff
personally.>*

From Maura
To Kristal

I get it. Kinda punishes Jacki and me though
'cuz you're pissed at Lynette.

From Kristal
To Maura

I know. I'm sorry.

...

...

From Maura
To Kristal

Would anything change your mind?

From Kristal
To Maura

<deleted: Not bloody likely>

...

<deleted: Doubt it>

...

Like what?

From Maura
To Kristal

I don't know.
If we all wore masks?
She might do it if Trent isn't around.
...

...

To protect Tabs.
...

...

Open windows? Filters?
Sleep on the porch like last summer?
I know you didn't have Tabby to worry about yet then,
but none of us came home with the crud.
...

All test before we come?

From Kristal
To Maura
I don't know.

...
...
...

From Maura
To Kristal

Let me just ask her.

From Kristal
To Maura

OK

From Maura
To Kristal

You're never gonna believe it
Just got off phone w/L. She's vaxxed AND boosted!
DON'T TELL TRENT!
L takes care of her aunt 2x/wk
said she "doesn't want to be the
one who kills her"

…

Will test ahead of time if you want :)
…

…

…

From Kristal
To Maura

<deleted: Vaxxed!?!? Doubt it!>

…

From Maura
To Kristal

Great Aunt Tillie.
L loves her
like a grandmother.

From Kristal
To Maura

<deleted: Vaxxed?!? Really???>

...

From Maura
To Kristal

We'll leave political talk at the door

From Kristal
To Maura

<deleted: Vaxxed AND boosted?
Without telling Trent???
Can I see her vax card?>

...

From Maura
To Kristal

If we let the orange one
come between us and our friend,
he wins, you know

...

From Maura
To Kristal

Please say yes

...

ODE TO MY BOOBS

By Jacqueline Sorenson
Writing as Jacki Zee
with apologies to Pablo Neruda and in homage to his poem,
"Ode to My Socks"

My divorce settlement bought me
a pair
of splendid hooters
which had eluded me my entire life.
Two breasts, plump
warm as August tomatoes.
I slipped them into my new sports bra
afraid they might
tumble
away
on
my morning run
all bounce
and jiggle.
Defiant jugs
they were
two flowered maracas
shaking out a rumba
with each even

footfall
two taut bongos
beating out my mambo
kettle drums
holding down the low end.
My chest
was honored
in this way
by
these
heavenly
snuggle pups.
They were
so handsome,
for the first time
the rest of my body seemed to me
unacceptable
ramshackle
all loose ligaments
flabby abs
drooping derriere
unworthy
of those triumphant mounds
those resplendent
orbs.

Nevertheless
I resisted
the sharp temptation
to save them for special occasions
like housewives of old,
china teacups and crystal goblets
tucked safely into hutches,
their husband's
mint corvette

under a gray blanket in the
garage.
I resisted
the mad impulse
to swaddle them
in wool and angora,
an extra layer of fleece.
Like our mothers and grandmothers who
freed their tatas
burned their bras
who claimed their bodies for
themselves,
I pulled on a silky, snug tee,
turned on
those magnificent headlights,
blinding anyone who dared to look.

The moral
of my ode is this:
beauty is twice
beauty
and what is good is doubly
good
when it is a matter of two new knockers
made of silicone
in your fifties.

NO POLITICS

CHARACTERS: Four women in their fifties - JACKI, KRISTAL, LYNETTE, MAURA

August, 2022, Night

A women's weekend at LYNETTE's rustic cabin. KRISTAL (optional: in a surgical mask), LYNETTE, and MAURA sprawl across plaid couches with wine glasses in various states of fullness.)

(Lights up.)

(Toilet flushes.)

(JACKI enters from an interior hallway with an empty wine glass, wearing a baggy University of Wisconsin sweatshirt and an unused tampon hanging from each ear. Swings her head around so the tampons fling around like a swing carousel at a carnival.)

JACKI: Hey girls, like my earrings?

KRISTAL: Oh my god. Where did you find those? It's been forever since I've had to deal with one of *those*.

> (JACKI spins one of the tampons on her index finger.)

JACKI: Heads up!

> (Flings it at LYNETTE almost knocking over LYNETTE's wine glass.)

> (LYNETTE snatches it from the air and slides it under her thigh.)

LYNETTE: Hailey and her friends must have left them when they were here in June.

> (LYNETTE grabs the other tampon from JACKI's ear and tucks it into her hoodie pocket. JACKI is refilling her wine glass and doesn't seem to notice.)

JACKI: Remember when we ordered the free samples from OB with the coupon on the back of the *Young Miss* magazine? I thought your mom was gonna split a gut when she walked in on us all trying to insert them!

MAURA: Oh my god! There we were with our shorts at our ankles and one foot on the toilet seat cover. (Gestures.) She probably thought it was some kind of Wiccan ritual or something.

JACKI: She always did think I was possessed.

KRISTAL: Well, who could blame her? The quilt you brought to sleepovers looked like a combination of a Georgia O'Keefe painting and Judy Chicago's *Dinner Party*.

JACKI: Yeah, yeah. Thank god, Mom didn't stay in her vagina quilting phase for very long. Remember how we joked that, if your dad happened upon us in the basement, he'd go back upstairs and jump your mom? Horny--but he wouldn't know why!

> (JACKI takes a big swig of wine and tops off her glass again. She moves to fill LYNETTE's but sees it's still full. Gestures that LYNETTE should drink up. LYNETTE lifts the glass to her lips, pretends to take a sip. Satisfied, JACKI returns to her own full glass.)

MAURA: Of course, I was in college before I realized what you meant by that. I thought they really *were* flowers.

JACKI: What?!?

MAURA: Seriously. I only pretended to know what you guys were talking about.

Believe it or not, I didn't have my first orgasm until I was 21. Guess that's what happens when you start out trying to have sex with the wrong gender.

LYNETTE: O-kay. We said we weren't going to talk politics this weekend—

KRISTAL: (Rolling her eyes.) Here we go...

JACKI: Honey, how in the world is Maura's being a lesbian "political" all of a sudden? You've known about it since we were in college.

KRISTAL: I've got a guess and he starts with the letter "T."

MAURA & JACKI: Whoa—hey—

JACKI: Now that *is* political. Can't we just—?

KRISTAL: Just what? I meant Trent, okay? Trent. Jeez. He's never liked Maura. It's a wonder he let Lynette invite her this weekend for god's sake.

(LYNETTE looks sheepish.)

JACKI: He does know she's *here*, doesn't he?

LYNETTE: (Hesitates.) Of course, he does. I mean I didn't tell him she *wasn't*

going to be here. She's always been
here before...
    (JACKI, KRISTAL, MAURA wait
    expectantly.)

LYNETTE: Okay, look, he didn't ask for
a guest list. I didn't give him one. And
Jacki's right. Who you have sex with
isn't political. Who *anybody* has sex with
isn't political. That's just been the
default mode around our place ever since—
well, you know. I'm sorry, you guys.

MAURA: That's okay. It can't be easy.

JACKI: Awww, Maur, you're such a peace-
maker. (Starts to say something else then
holds her tongue.)

MAURA: Let's move on.

JACKI: Good idea. Hey, you guys, remember
our bust-enhancing exercises? (Starts to
pump her arms to the chant.) We must, we
must, we must increase the bust!

    (KRISTAL, MAURA, and JACKI look
    expectantly at LYNETTE who is
    not participating.)

KRISTAL: The bigger the better!

MAURA: The tighter the sweater!

    (KRISTAL, MAURA, and JACKI look expectantly at LYNETTE who is not participating.)

LYNETTE: (Reluctantly lifts her arms and gives a pump.) The boys depend on us!

TOGETHER: They do. They do. They do. They do! (ALL laughing except LYNETTE.)

    (KRISTAL, MAURA, and JACKI repeat the rhyme.)

JACKI: (Drains her wine glass and pretends to hear someone calling her.) Hear that? It's the lake calling. Must be time for The Dip. Guess it's time for you guys to check out my new boobs!

KRISTAL: You didn't!

JACKI: I did. Last one in is a rotten egg. (Takes off her sweatshirt and exits.)

KRISTAL: You heard her.

    (KRISTAL goes down the hall and returns with a stack of towels.)

KRISTAL: You'll thank me for these later. Come on, you guys. (Exits.)

MAURA: (Starts to stand.) No use fighting it. You coming?

LYNETTE: You go ahead. I'll pee and meet you down there.

MAURA: Hey, don't let that whole thing bother you.

LYNETTE: It's not that...

MAURA: Then what is it?

LYNETTE: Nothing. I'm fine. Let's join them. (Does NOT move to stand. She is obviously NOT fine.)

MAURA: Come on. Well? Out with it?

LYNETTE: I can't... I don't... (Pulls a tampon from her pocket, fiddles with it while she summons up the resolve to tell MAURA.) These aren't Hailey's. They're mine. Or at least they were.

MAURA: Wait, what? You're *still* getting your period? That can't be normal.

LYNETTE: Yeah, well, no. It's not *normal-normal* but the doctor said I don't need to worry about it. Not yet.

MAURA: So that's good. (Starts to take off her shoes and socks.) Bummer about your period though. Is that why you don't want to take The Dip? (Changes to a comedic voice.) Are ya "on the rag?"

      (LYNETTE starts to fidget, cry, looks
      nervous, embarrassed, evasive.)

LYNETTE: I wish. I haven't gotten my
period for two months. (Seems to want
to confide in MAURA then thinks better
of it.) I'm sorry. Just forget about it.

MAURA: Wait. I'm having trouble tracking
here, hon. First, you're upset because
you haven't gone through menopause yet,
and now you're complaining because
you skipped a period? Celebrate! Have
another drink!

      (MAURA takes a big swallow of wine,
      watches as LYNETTE *doesn't* drink.)

LYNETTE: My breasts are tender. I'm nau-
seous all the time...

MAURA: You don't think—?

LYNETTE: Yeah, I do. And I know you're
the last person I should be dumping this
on after all you... I'm so sorry.

      (MAURA contemplates the situation.)

MAURA: Okay. Stop. We shouldn't freak
out until we know for sure. We'll just
go into town and get you a test and—

LYNETTE: I have a test in my suitcase,
but I'm afraid to take it.

MAURA: Well, you go right in there, Missy, and pee on that stick. We're not going to get all freaked out until we know what you're dealing with.

LYNETTE: But—?

MAURA: No buts. Go!

> (LYNETTE exits. MAURA settles in
> to wait.)

MAURA: (Talking up to be heard in the other room.) Remember when Jacki had that scare our junior year? That turned out to be nothing. And she was almost three months late.

LYNETTE: (From inside.) Yeah, and this is what got Kristal married to Brett. They *never* would have gotten married if she hadn't gotten pregnant.

MAURA: Well, yeah, but that turned out okay.

> (Sound of toilet flushing and
> water running.)

MAURA: They're probably the happiest straight couple I know.

> (LYNETTE returns with pregnancy
> test and box in hand. Sets them on

the coffee table and starts the timer
on her phone.)

LYNETTE: I'm not in my twenties with my
whole life ahead of me. Hailey and Rachel
could make me a grandmother any time now.
It's embarrassing. Not to mention dangerous. The probability of birth defects...
the mortality rate for pregnant women my
age is... (Pause.) Maur, I'm scared.

MAURA: I know you are. You haven't told
Trent I assume?

LYNETTE: God, no. He'll kill me. Not
kill-kill, but you know what I mean.

MAURA: Well, if you *are* pregnant—and we
don't know that yet—it's not like you got
that way all by yourself. Why would he—?

LYNETTE: Here's the thing. (Pause.) Trent
got a vasectomy years ago.

MAURA: Wait, what? Then who? (Pauses
to think about it, smiles.) I know I
shouldn't be smiling, but, Lynnie, did
you take a lover?

LYNETTE: Oh, Lord, no. It was just the
one time.

MAURA: One time? Jeez. Who?

LYNETTE: Here's where it gets real bad. (Long pause.) It was our new pastor.

MAURA: (Quashes a big reaction.) Did he—?
LYNETTE: No. It was completely consensual. Well, mostly. Yes. Completely. I could have said no at any time. We agreed afterwards. Only the once. It was nice though. Spontaneous. He's a little younger. No delay for a pill to kick in. No *pretending* to enjoy it. So different to have someone want me and care about my—what felt good. (Pause.) You had your first orgasm at 21. (Pause.) I had my first *real* one a couple months ago.

(MAURA reacts with surprise.)

LYNETTE: And this is my punishment. Fifty-five years old and I'm going to die in childbirth. If Trent doesn't kill me first.

MAURA: Don't talk like that. (Starts to go into problem solving mode.) He never needs to know. Why don't you come home to Chicago with me for a few days? We still have choices down there...in case you...if you decide...

(LYNETTE holds up her hand to stop her.)

LYNETTE: No politics.

MAURA: Honey, I'm not talking about politics. Men have made it seem like it's about politics. I'm talking about your life. Your one and *only* life.
LYNETTE: Don't I know it?

(The timer on LYNETTE's phone sounds. JACKI and KRISTAL return laughing, wearing towels, shivering, and dripping wet from the lake. LYNETTE and MAURA exchange worried glances. JACKI and KRISTAL towel off their hair. LYNETTE hands the test stick to MAURA without looking at it and exits to her bedroom.)

JACKI: You missed it. Colder than a witch's tit but my new ones were smokin' hot!

(MAURA looks at the test stick, holds it out to the others. They look at it and react.)

CURTAIN

PRAYER BANK OF AMERICA

May the Lord answer your prayers
out of the depth of His love for you.

ORIGINAL ONLINE PRAYER REQUEST:

Prayer for Restored Fertility
by Trent T. 5/10/2008

Some years ago, I faltered in my trust in the LORD and had a vasectomy. There, I said it. My wife and I were in some financial hot water, and I was afraid we couldn't afford more children. I regretted my surgery almost immediately. Even though I could have had a procedure to *try* to reverse it, I heard it was incredibly painful (and expensive) and felt this would be another betrayal of GOD and his WILL. Plus, I looked it up: vasectomies fail 1 in 10,000 times. Those are better than the odds of getting attacked by a shark (and that happens all the time!). The way I see it, if the LORD wants me to be a father again, He will surely make it happen. He just needs a nudge toward "wanting."

Today, we watched my youngest walk across the stage at her graduation from technical college. I know this sort of feeling is usually reserved for women when their biological clocks are ticking, but, being in that auditorium at the "end of an era" as my wife called it, I had this overwhelming urge to be a father once again. That is why I am asking for your prayers today, to help me show the LORD how sorry I am and to ask His forgiveness and beg Him to bless me with a son. For obvious reasons, this is something I can't ask for at my church. Plus I know what our pastor would say. Thank you for your prayers.

Update 09/08/2008

Many thanks to the 312 people who have prayed for me. When I posted my prayer request, I thought it would turn out like Jennifer S's with only 3 people trying to intercede with the LORD, but 312?!? Even if I never have another child, the gift of your prayers has shown me GOD's love. Thank you!

Update 01/01/2009

Thank you for the 547 prayers on my behalf. Still no baby but I haven't given up hope. The LORD will provide.

Update 06/09/2009

Still no baby but I haven't given up hope. How could I, with over 600 people praying for me? I hope my prayers on your behalf are working for you, too. I always look for the requests that have the least number of prayer responses. I figure those people need my prayers more than the others. I hope you'll understand if I don't get to your prayers.

Update 01/05/2010

Thank you all for your prayers. My wife still hasn't conceived. Not for lack of trying on my part if you know what I mean. Ha. Ha. But seriously, I can't believe it has been almost two whole years since I first posted to this site. I'm so grateful for your kind prayers. I don't know what God's ideal number is, but maybe if one thousand people talk to him on my behalf, he can't ignore them, right? I hope so. That seems like a good goal for me. I'm laid up with the flu today and will offer up a few more prayers than usual on your behalf, too. Blessed be.

Update 06/01/2010

Another whole year has passed and still no baby, but after my last update, I noticed that my number of prayers increased, so I'm going to try to give updates more often.

Update 07/01/2010

Still no baby but thank you for your prayers.

Update 08/01/2010

Still no baby but thank you for your prayers.

Update 09/10/2010

This will be my last update for a while. There is still no baby, but thank you, Roy S, for your side message letting me know the etiquette of posting updates. From now on, I'll only post when something develops. In the meantime, I will continue to pray for you all. Yours in CHRIST, Trent T.

Update 05/14/2017

It seems that the window for my prayer to be answered might be closing. Please pray that I have the strength to avoid the temptation of the little blue pill. Surely, if the LORD wanted me to be a father again, HE could make that happen without pharmacuticals (sp?) but also, HE gave us the power to invent them, so maybe HE wants us to use them. See what I mean about temptation? I thought about seeking counsel from our pastor, but I know what he'd say. Oh, LORD, lead me not into temptation. Amen.

Update 08/10/2018

Today is my wife's 50th birthday, so I should probably give up my wish for another child. Come to think of it, I probably should have given it up a long time ago. Even if she could get pregnant, it would probably be dangerous for her—and the baby, too. I guess. Many thanks to the 1,733 people who have lifted up your prayers for me over the past 10 years. Ten years! I feel like I know you in a way that I don't even know the people in my church. Please pray that I can find peace knowing that GOD doesn't see fit to bless me with a son. Maybe it's his punishment for not trusting him in the first place. I must trust HIS WISDOM now. I will continue to pray for you all.

Update 01/17/2022

I'm baaaack! I bet you didn't expect to hear from me again. Today I had a conversation with our new pastor. I swear the guy is like truth serum or something. I spilled my guts about everything, and (can you believe it?) he didn't rip me a new one (pardon my French) for doubting GOD's WILL. Instead, he shared all kinds of scripture about women in the Bible who had late-in-life pregnancies. Sara, Rebekah, Elisabet, Rachel, to name a few. Our oldest daughter is named Rachel. Is that a sign? Anyway, he told me not to give up hope! "If you want to have more children, you have every right to pray and ask others to pray for you," he said. I asked him to pray for me but told him I wasn't ready to ask for the prayers of the whole congregation just yet. So if you can find it in your hearts to storm the heavens on my behalf one more time, I would be eternally grateful. Yours in CHRIST, Trent T.

Update 09/05/2022

(Labor Day!) GOD is GREAT! Today I learned that my wife is with child. I trust GOD's infinite GOODNESS to protect her and my son. It must be a son. I can feel it. We haven't had an ultrasound to find out yet. Maybe he will go on to do something very special with his life. Maybe even change the world. I can never thank you enough–all 2,384 of you–for lifting up your prayers on my behalf. I am rich beyond measure.

"You will keep in perfect peace those whose minds are steadfast, because they trust in YOU. Trust in the LORD forever, for the LORD, the LORD himself, is the ROCK ETERNAL." –Isaiah 26:3-4

IN MEMORIAM

LYNETTE MARIE (WILSON) THOMPSON, 55, of Frazier, WI, was called to her Heavenly Home on March 15, 2023, from complications of childbirth.

Lynette was born on August 10, 1968, to Jeffrey and Veronica Wilson in Frazier. After graduating from Rock Ridge Unified High School in 1987, she went on to study Communications at the University of Wisconsin at Whitewater. She made the Dean's List every semester of her college career and graduated with honors.

After graduation, she married Trent William Thompson, and stayed home to raise their two daughters, Hailey and Rachel, who were the light of her life. Their friends often called Lynette "Mom," and the Thompson house was the gathering place for them in their teen years. Her chocolate chip cookies were legendary, and there was always room at the dinner table for an extra visitor or two.

Lynette was active in New Hope Bible Church, singing in the choir and serving meals to the less fortunate. Every year, she directed the Christmas Eve pageant, which became more professional and elaborate with each passing year, "for the glory of God," she always said. For many years, she was an active caregiver for her great aunt, Tillie Wilson.

One of Lynette's favorite pastimes was entertaining friends and family at their cabin in Northern Wisconsin. She was especially grateful to have one last visit there with her lifelong friends, Jacki Sorenson, Kristal Moore, and Maura McElroy, the summer before she passed.

Lynette was predeceased by her father, Jeffrey, her grandparents, Steven and Marcy Wilson and Bruce and Angela Burke. She is survived by her mother, Veronica; great aunt Tillie; brothers, Anthony, Frank, and Charles; her husband, Trent; her daughters, Hailey Marie and Rachel Susan; and son, Trent William, Jr.

A visitation will be held at New Hope Bible Church on Friday, March 24, 2023, at 1:00 p.m. followed by a funeral service at 2:30 p.m.

In lieu of flowers, the family asks that donations be made to the Prader-Willi Syndrome Association.

UNAUTHORIZED

CHARACTERS: Three women in their fifties – JACKI, KRISTAL (optional: wearing a surgical mask), MAURA. They're all dressed for a funeral with dress boots and wool dress coats.

March 2023, Night

(Dim lights come up on a darkened cabin. The light of cell phones shine through the windows in the door. There is laughing and bumping around on the porch. The sound of a loud thump/crash on the other side of the cabin stops the murmuring on the porch.)

KRISTAL: (Tipsy, banging on the door from the porch.) You okay in there?

> (More rustling around. Women on the
> porch struggle to see in the window.
> Indirect light shows in the hallway
> off the living room. The two voices
> on the porch are getting impatient.)

KRISTAL: We can't just keep looking for
the key under the flowerpot, NOOOOOO.
Jacki has to be a hero.

MAURA: It's not there. How many different
ways can we look for it? Trent probably left it in his pocket when he got
the call.

> (MAURA and KRISTAL ad lib "look-
> ing-for-it" lines and actions.)

MAURA: (Banging.) Come on, Jacki. Open
up. We've gotta pee out here.

> (Toilet flushes. JACKI appears, tri-
> umphant, drying her hands on her
> pants and flicks on the light. There
> is a small cut above one eye. Her
> hair is mussed. She, too, is tip-
> sy--a bit more tipsy than KRISTAL.)

JACKI: Yeah, yeah. Here I come.

> (Opens the door.)

KRISTAL: Thank, God!

(Rushes past JACKI, leaves an 8x10 framed photograph face down on the coffee table and makes for the bathroom.)

(MAURA hands JACKI a huge purse that has a Nalgene water bottle peeking out the top of it. MAURA sets down a grocery bag and pulls out its contents: 4 bottles of wine (one which is half-empty), an empty pint bottle of spirits, a bag of chips and one of peanut M&Ms.)

(JACKI grabs the wine bottle, takes a swig, and screws on the lid.)

MAURA: Good thing the snow has already started to melt up here. Would have been a long hoof up an unplowed driveway in these.

(She takes off her dress boots, starts to take off her coat but thinks better of it. Puts her boots back on. Begins to build a fire in the fireplace.)

JACKI: Yeah, good thing Trent didn't think to shut down the water after he got the news—

(Stops abruptly. Uncomfortable silence.)

Shit, it's cold in here.

(Grabs a throw from the back of a chair and wraps up in it. Heads for the kitchen.)

(Toilet flushes. KRISTAL returns drying her hands on her pants.)

(JACKI returns with wine glasses and a serving bowl.)

KRISTAL: (To MAURA.) Your turn. Stop at the linen closet on your way and grab a hand towel.

(KRISTAL picks up the fire preparation where MAURA left off.)

(MAURA scoots off to the bathroom while JACKI pours three generous glasses of wine, retrieves the bag of chips, opens and pours them into the bowl. Grabs a few for herself. Opens the M&Ms and hands a glass to KRISTAL.)

KRISTAL: We didn't have to build too many of these in August. Just that one year.

(JACKI hands her a glass and they drink. KRISTAL finishes building the fire and lights it while the dialogue continues.)

JACKI: Yeah, everything was weird that year. Oh, God, remember? She was pregnant with Hailey and was afraid to take The Dip. Thought she'd shock the baby or some dumb thing.

KRISTAL: Hey, don't make fun. We all had weird paranoias with our first kids. Once I called the doctor to see if it was okay to go to an Elton John concert. I was worried Jeremy would be born with hearing loss or some ridiculous thing. And the doctor, to her great credit, didn't laugh right out loud. Although, now that I think about it, there was a period of silence where she was probably covering up the mouthpiece and laughing her ass off...

JACKI: (Pulls a bag of gummies from her purse.) Look what I brought!

KRISTAL: Geez. You're like Mary Poppins. What else you got in that bag?

(KRISTAL starts to peek in her purse and JACKI cuts her off.)

JACKI: Patience, grasshopper. Be a good girl and I'll let you see later.

(JACKI opens the bag and offers it to KRISTAL who takes one and starts chewing. JACKI pops one into her mouth, too.)

KRISTAL: Where'd you get these? Your students?

JACKI: Not even close, but that would be funny.

    (KRISTAL notices the photo on the coffee table and moves aside the other family photos on the mantle to give the portrait of Lynette the place of honor.)

KRISTAL: There. That's better.

    (MAURA returns and trades her coat for a throw.)

MAURA: Mmm. Nice fire.

    (JACKI silently offers MAURA a gummy. MAURA holds up her hand to refuse. JACKI holds the bag out to her again.)

JACKI: C'mon. For old time's sake. Better than passing around a joint. Covid, y'know.

    (MAURA takes one and starts chewing. Catches sight of KRISTAL straightening Lynette's picture.)

MAURA: Aw, Lynnie...

    (THEY ALL pause and sigh.)

JACKI: (Wipes a tear then shakes it off, picks up a glass and hands it to MAURA.) All right, Maur, you are far too sober. Thanks for driving by the way.

MAURA: No problem. It seemed the safest alternative.

KRISTAL: Well, we appreciate it. (Holds up her glass.) To our driver!

MAURA: No, the first drink needs to be to Lynnie.

KRISTAL: Of course.

JACKI, KRISTAL, MAURA: To Lynnie.

    (THEY ALL toast.)

KRISTAL: It's so weird being in this place without her.

MAURA: Yeah, but she'd love the fact that we're here together.

JACKI: Yeah, except for the broken screen and the lamp that bit the dust on my way in.

    (THEY ALL laugh and start to settle in for a visit. Grabbing handfuls of snacks and taking drinks of wine. EACH finds something to snuggle under.)

MAURA: *That's* what that was. I hope it wasn't the fish lamp.

KRISTAL: Yeah, she'd never forgive you for that. Where's that picture of her with the fish lamp? I blew it up and sent it to her.

> (Starts looking through the albums on a shelf, leafs through the pages stopping occasionally to admire a picture, sighs and laughs, here and there.)

MAURA: (Notices the cut above JACKI's eye.) Looks like you got a dinger.

> (JACKI touches the cut, sees blood on her finger, grabs a tissue, and holds it over her eye, not making anything of it.)

> (KRISTAL starts to laugh louder.)

> (JACKI & MAURA exchange a glance.)

JACKI: Honey, it's not *that* funny and the gummy couldn't have kicked in *that* fast. Of course, you always were a lightweight.

> (KRISTAL can't contain herself. It's the kind of laugh-until-you-cry that happens after a funeral.)

KRISTAL: Oh, god, I know. I'm sorry. It's not funny at all. (Laughs some more.)

JACKI: (Starting to feel insulted.) Well, you don't have to laugh so hard then...

KRISTAL: I'm sorry. It's just—I can't stop picturing the look on Trent's face when he realizes her picture is missing. What's he going to say?

JACKI: Well, I, for one, don't give a flying fuck what he says. I'm still pissed at him for that lame-ass obituary.

> (JACKI begins a rant that the other two have listened to for the past two hours in the car. THEY ALL take drinks of wine and wait out the storm.)

JACKI: I mean where the hell was Lynnie in the whole thing? That obit could have been written about ANYbody—EH-NEE-BAH-DEE—in their whole congregation—well, any *woman* in that whole congregation anyway. How many men are directing the nativity play and baking chocolate chip cookies for the whole neighborhood? A monkey—

KRISTAL & MAURA: (In unison.) Could have done a better job!

(KRISTAL & MAURA laugh and clink glasses. Take a drink. KRISTAL starts to pull herself together.)

MAURA: Well, we did get a mention at least.

KRISTAL: I bet the girls shamed Trent into that.

MAURA: It's better than nothing.

JACKI: Hardly. (Takes a drink.) And what about that pastor? (Mocking.) "Lynette was a god-fearing woman." "God called her home." "God's will." "God. God. God." Jee-zus! It was like he'd never laid eyes on her before.

MAURA: (Under her breath.) I wish. (Grabs a handful of snacks and shoves them in her mouth.)

(KRISTAL notices MAURA's discomfort and catches her eye, but MAURA shrugs her off.)

KRISTAL: The woman has a point. (Takes another drink.) There wasn't one thing in that eulogy that showed the real Lynette. At least who she was *before*.

(THEY ALL continue to take drinks and eat snacks while talking.)

JACKI: (Laughing.) I'd love to see the looks on their holier-than-thou faces if we'd told them how much she liked swimming in the raw. Well, when she wasn't pregnant, anyway. Oh, and what about that time she made us go to the Chippendales knock-off show in the Dells?

    (MAURA is still distracted and doesn't respond.)

KRISTAL: Oh my god! I wish we had a picture of *that*, the dollar bill in her mouth trying to catch the eye of the dark-haired guy on the other side of the stage.

    (KRISTAL is losing it again.)

And that blonde guy who wouldn't leave her alone.

    (Mimics his gestures trying to turn on Lynette.)

JACKI: Yeah, she *said* she hated it but I don't know...

KRISTAL: Okay, so skinny dipping, Chippendales. What else would we put in the unauthorized eulogy?

    (THEY ALL think for a beat.)

KRISTAL: We'd have to include something about sledding on the lunch trays she pinched from the cafeteria in college—

JACKI: And getting busted by her boss when she took them back after hours.

KRISTAL: Couldn't just drop them by the back door and leave them there. Noooo, she had to go in and wash them and put them back where they belonged. Always had to make things "right." Whatever *that* was.

JACKI: Yeah, she was always big on right and wrong. Probably how that church of Trent's got its hooks into her and sucked all the fun out.

KRISTAL: Life's so much easier when it's black and white. (Takes a drink.) And you're white.

> (MAURA's throat catches a sob. The others notice. Pause.)

JACKI. (To MAURA.) Honey, what would you want to put in her eulogy?

MAURA: (Shakes her head but can't answer.)

JACKI: Maybe something about the summer you had that sublet together?

MAURA: (Starts to pull herself together.) I hadn't thought about that but (Considers.) yeah. I'd say something about how nice it was to come home from the restaurant to a bowl of freshly-popped popcorn and a glass of lavender iced tea, which sounds weird but it really was nice. (Starts to laugh.) We'd watch reruns of *Golden Girls* of all things. And we'd joke about which of us would be which one of them when we got old. Jacki, you, of course, would be Blanche.

JACKI: And you're Dorothy.

MAURA: Naturally. (Smiles.) We'd argue about whether she'd end up being Rose or Dorothy's mom. What was her name?

Kristal: Sophia

MAURA: (Laughs through tears.) Sophia. She always hated it when I suggested she'd end up like Sophia. She'd say, "Shoot me if I ever live to be that old."

(THEY ALL look at the portrait.)

MAURA: And now... How I wish... (Takes a long drink.)

KRISTAL: I know. (Moves to comfort her.)

MAURA: What about you? What would you have put in her eulogy?

KRISTAL: Well, before she got all swallowed up by her MAGA-loving husband, she really was a good friend. Remember when I cracked up my parents' car that summer after senior year, and I was scared to go home by myself?

JACKI: How you didn't see the tree is beyond me.

KRISTAL: Those were the days when my dad's drinking was really bad, and I never knew what he'd do from minute to minute, but I did know—or at least I hoped—he'd manage to keep a lid on it as long as Lynnie was around. He loved her. Probably had a little crush on her if I had to guess. Nothing gross or anything. He just always perked up when she was around. Anyway, when I was about to break it to my parents that the car had a collapsed front end, Lynnie chimed in, said *she* was driving, that she'd *begged* me to let her drive home, and the accident had been all her fault.

MAURA: Seriously? She lied for you? That girl hated to lie.

JACKI: (In a prissy voice.) *I'd rather die than lie.*

KRISTAL: I know. She made me promise not to tell anyone, too. I still got in trouble for letting someone else drive their car, but you should have seen how forgiving he was of her. I didn't know he had it in him.

MAURA: Yeah, she had that way about her.

JACKI: And you kept your promise not to tell until now. What else are you keeping from us? Hm?

KRISTAL: Nothing. Well, you knew she got cold feet on her wedding day. That's no secret.

JACKI: Yup, old news. I wish she'd have listened to her gut on that one. What about you, Maur? Anything you're holding out on us?

    (MAURA hesitates, takes another drink, thinks.)

MAURA: I never told you guys, but, when I turned forty, Jillian and I tried and tried to get pregnant. Sperm donor and all that. I don't know why I told Lynette and not you—maybe I wanted to convince her that our relationship was just like theirs. She didn't make it a secret that she and Trent struggled to conceive at first, too. Anyway, in retrospect, it's probably a good thing we never got pregnant. I'd be raising a child by myself and—oh my god, the kid would be in high school by now—weird. A couple more years and we'd—I'd—have an empty nest—

JACKI: (Making a buzzer sound like in a game show.) Doesn't qualify. You're telling us something we didn't know about *you*—I *am* sorry about not being able to get pregnant by the way. That totally sucks. I mean that. What about something we don't know about *her*?

MAURA: I'm getting to that. (Takes a drink.) She felt so bad for me that, without thinking about it, she blurted out, "Let me be a surrogate." We both knew there was no possibility in the world that Trent would ever allow that, that it would ever fly in her church to carry a baby for a couple of lesbians, but...well, her desire to help me was so genuine and spontaneous. I knew—at least *then*—she really did get that our relationship was a real marriage. When Jillian walked out, Lynnie sent me a beautiful card and flowers.

(THEY ALL drink and reflect.)

KRISTAL: She really would have given anyone the shirt off her back.

JACKI: Okay, I know I'm going to sound like a total bee-atch, but we really do have to get past this cult of self-sacrifice bullshit as a measurement of women. It drives me nuts. You know what I wish people knew about Lynnie? I wish they knew she wasn't always the adoring, cookie-baking, altar-banner-sewing martyr that pastor made her out to be. That one day she dropped off her kids at her mother's house and flew the coop.

> (KRISTAL and MAURA react but don't interrupt the story.)

JACKI: I know, right? I've just given my last final of the semester and am headed for my car when who's there but Lynnie, wearing a gray sweatshirt with a stain on it and one of Trent's baseball caps. Grandma is on duty until Sunday night and Trent's up here with his fishing buddies. He's been gone for a week, and she's bouncing off the walls. Remember how those kids were such horrible sleepers when they were toddlers? Anyway, her eyes look like they're going to fall right out of her head she's so exhausted. I take her back to my place and she sleeps the sleep of the dead—

> (JACKI's voice catches and they all look at the photo, take a drink.)

JACKI: (Sniffs.) Next day she wakes up all refreshed. We have brunch and go to the Farmer's Market and shopping on State Street, and she lets me buy her a sassy sundress and some strappy sandals, and we have a beer at the Union Terrace, and she looks ten years younger than she did the day before. We even go out dancing and some dude hits on her. You should have seen the light in her eyes, like she was a different person. That's how I want to remember her.

KRISTAL: Yeah, that's way better than—here it is!

> (Holds up a photo of a young Lynette pretending to French kiss a taxi-dermied fish that is part of a lamp.)

JACKI: Oh my god. I can't believe she left that here where anyone could find it. I bet Trent would have a conniption.

MAURA: Aw, look at her.

> (Places it on the mantle next to the portrait.)

KRISTAL: She looks so much like Hailey. Or Hailey looks like her. Isn't it weird to think that young thing would go on to have two kids—

MAURA: Three.

KRISTAL: Oh, god, of course. Three. How is Trent going to raise that baby all by himself?

JACKI: I know this is worse than awful, but a part of me feels like it serves him right.

(MAURA and KRISTAL react with shock.)

JACKI: I *said* it was worse than awful. I just can't forgive him for getting her knocked up, putting her in such jeopardy, knowing that abortion wouldn't be an option. I mean, he couldn't—

MAURA: They.

JACKI: Fine, *they* couldn't use protection? I say, if a guy doesn't want his partner to have an abortion, he should get himself fixed. It's the least he could have done.

MAURA: He did.

KRISTAL: Did what?

MAURA: Got himself "fixed" as you so delicately put it.

JACKI: You have *got* to be kidding.

(MAURA shakes her head.)

JACKI: Then how—?

KRISTAL: I've heard things can grow back together.

JACKI: Where do you get your information, girl? A seventh grader?

KRISTAL: No, seriously there's like a 1% failure rate. The doctor made Brett go back to check his sperm count after he healed up to be sure. Maybe Trent never did the follow—

MAURA: I'm pretty sure it took.

JACKI: Maur, what aren't you telling us?

MAURA: (To the picture.) Aw, Lynnie. (To KRISTAL and JACKI.) Lynnie made me promise not to tell anyone. (Hesitates.) Trent isn't the biological father.

JACKI & KRISTAL: Whaaat?!?

MAURA: One time. She told me she had sex with someone else one time.

> (More shocked reactions from JACKI & KRISTAL.)

MAURA: She made me promise not to tell anyone. Was resigned to having the baby, hoping it would be a boy—for Trent. God. I can't... I knew and I didn't do anything about it.

KRISTAL: What were you supposed to *do*, honey?

JACKI: More importantly, who *is* the father?

(MAURA, shaking her head, can't answer. KRISTAL moves to comfort her.)

MAURA: It was that damned pastor.

JACKI: You have got to be fucking kidding me!

KRISTAL: Are you sure? How do you know?

JACKI: Honestly, I'm not surprised. Okay, I am from Lynnie's point of view—what a dud—but it doesn't surprise me that that slimy bastard would take advantage—I bet he raped her.

MAURA: (Shrugs.) She *said* it was consensual, but there's still the question of his position. I'm still kicking myself—

KRISTAL: Well, you stop that right now. You didn't cause any of this. But we do need to figure out what to do with this information. Trent is raising someone else's child—

JACKI: And Pastor Can't-Keep-His-Dick-In-His-Pants'll do this to someone else. We need to nail his balls to the wall.

KRISTAL: The least he should do is pay for little TJ'S care. With Prader-Willi, he's going to need it.

JACKI: There's no way to make the pastor pay his dues without letting Trent in on the baby's parentage. The guy'll go ape shit.

MAURA: And the person who could call out the "man of God" on abusing his position is — she's gone. I've played this out through my head a million times. A DNA test would show the baby is his, but there'd be no proof that Lynnie didn't initiate the — it wasn't even a relationship. I guess a paternity suit would make him pay the bills, but—

> (Long period of silence while they all consider.)

JACKI: Aaaaaand here we are again, letting this whole issue revolve around the men. You know, that baby is half Lynnie's, too. (Takes another drink and refills her glass and drinks again.) And the man who has been with her for her entire adult life has a responsibility to that half, whether he provided the sperm or not. And don't even tell me Trent never strayed in all those years of marriage. Well, even if he didn't, doesn't their church teach about forgiveness?

> (MAURA and KRISTAL listen but don't seem convinced.)

KRISTAL: Who is going to love that baby like he needs to be loved?

JACKI: That baby has grown sisters who can help. And us aunties. Hell, I'm not above extorting money out of Pastor McDick—

KRISTAL: I'm not sure Lynnie would want—

JACKI: Okay, fine, maybe not.

> (Takes a long drink of wine. More silence while they all consider, each woman in her own head considering what to do, starting to talk then stopping, etc.)

JACKI: (Contemplating the photo of Lynette kissing the fish.) Tell you what. Let's figure out what Lynnie would want tomorrow. (Finishes the wine in her glass.) Right now, you know what *I* want?

KRISTAL: What?

JACKI: I want to take one last dip with our old friend.

> (Walks over to her purse and extracts her water bottle, which is filled half-way with powder.)

JACKI: (To the bottle.) What do ya say, Lynnie? How about a dip for old time's sake?

KRISTAL: What the—?

MAURA: How did you—?

JACKI: Are you kidding? A room full of grieving people? All you need to do is act like you're completing an assigned task and no one questions it. I felt a little bad about doing the transfer in a bathroom stall but...

KRISTAL: That's not all of her? You left some...?

JACKI: Yes, I left some for Trent. I'm not completely without shame. He'll never miss this.

MAURA: You do know the lake is still frozen.

JACKI: Of course. We're going to sprinkle her on top of the snow and let her melt in with the spring thaw. She was always one to ease in instead of jumping off the dock anyway.

KRISTAL: I bet there are some old boots around here, maybe some jackets.

> (KRISTAL rustles around in the closet.)

JACKI: Remember her trying to keep her boobs above the water's surface until the last possible moment?

> (Mimes someone timidly entering a cold lake. KRISTAL reappears with over-sized winter clothing and starts doling it out.)

(MAURA & JACKI laugh and they all start pulling on boots, coats, and hats.)

MAURA: Oh, and when she was pregnant...

(Holds an imaginary pregnant belly while she holds her hand up in the air trying to bounce from toe to toe to keep her chest above the surface of the water.)

(ALL laughing at MAURA, resume bundling up and then look up at each other in the ridiculous, too-big winter gear and start laughing again.)

(JACKI fills their glasses one more time and they move to toast.)

JACKI: (To the portrait.) Don't worry, Lynnie. We'll take care of things.

MAURA & KRISTAL: To Lynnie!

(They all drink down their glasses. JACKI picks up the water bottle and puts up her hood and heads for the door. The others snug up their coats and follow her. MAURA stops to turn off the light and look back at the room. A soft light illuminates the picture of Lynnie kissing the fish.)

CURTAIN

ERADICATED

ERADICATED

Artism: disorder which seizes its victims with the unnatural desire to create artifacts that disturb the view and provide nothing of practical use.

—*Diagnostic and Statistical Manual of Mental Disorders*
(DSM-9-TR)

I don't know what it was exactly: the impulse toward rebellion in the face of conformity, some primitive fascination with the use of hands, who can say? But suddenly in the winter of my forty-ninth year, I was seized with an intense urge to seek out the company of artists. Artists. Paint-spattered, t-shirt-wearing, clay-under-the-fingernails, collage-making artists. I wanted to hang out with people and ask, "What's your medium?" And say things like, "That's so derivative."

In my research, I had read descriptions of the colonies, set off deep in the woods, high on mountaintops, perched in hidden places where the land was too rocky or depleted to provide food. Following the explosion of computer-generated artwork, the artists, already dwindling in numbers, were now all but gone. I wanted desperately to see them before they breathed their last, before their disease was completely eradicated, and they became a mere footnote in the DSM. I wanted to see them before we could claim victory by quarantining Artism's victims and destroying the products of their disturbed minds.

At first, many in the mental health field objected to the deception, argued that it was cruel to pretend that the sufferers' work was being sold in exchange for room, board, and unlimited time to create it. But then, the afflicted started to admit themselves to the colonies. And the psychiatry community saw victory within reach.

I arrived on December 21st, my small suitcase in the trunk of a rental vehicle, my fully-charged tablet on the front seat. The warden—no, that was not the term I was to use—the Executive Director, Dr. Phelps, greeted me with a smile and a handshake. Her warm brown eyes and single dimple reminded me of Miss Ellefsen, my teacher for the first half of second grade. I'd not thought of Miss E. for over forty years, and her memory both unsettled and warmed me.

"Good of you to come, Dr. Bells." She led me toward the utilitarian building, ironic considering all the creative people it had housed over the years. Maybe that was the point. As we walked to her office, she sounded like a tour guide rattling off the institution's amenities and statistics. "We have almost completed our purpose. No new admits in five years. Consolidating our population with those of other facilities as the buildings get repurposed. It looks like the quarantine worked beyond our most optimistic projections."

I could tell from the set of her shoulders she was proud of her work. The fact that she'd commuted the two hours from home on her day off to show me around was a testament to her pride. That, or the hope of a mention by name in my report. Executive Directors weren't above that sort of thing.

"Yes, I needed to see for myself." I followed her up the steps. "Not that I doubted other research findings, of course. I guess I'm like the people who wanted to see the glaciers before they disappeared. Something to tell the kids about."

She showed me into her office. "How old are your kids?" On the credenza behind her, an electronic picture frame scrolled through photos of a set of toddler triplets.

"Oh, no, I don't actually have kids of my own."

Her brow furrowed.

"I mean that more in the figurative sense, as in future generations. Those who don't know history are doomed to repeat it. That kind of thing."

"Ah. Well." She gestured to a clear space on the floor. "You can leave your things here. I'll give you a tour."

I followed her to an airy common room. A patient—Phelps called her a "guest"—in gray scrubs stood behind an easel. Her white frizzy hair was piled on top of her head, a smear of yellow paint running from her right temple to her chin. She peered intently at another patient, stiff on an aqua-colored plastic chair. This patient—no, guest—also clad in gray, had her hands tied behind her. A black bandana blindfolded her eyes, and a dingy rag had been stuffed into her mouth. For the quickest moment, I thought the hospital was having some sort of hostage incident. Then I realized the "hostage" was the subject of the painting, a live model.

"That's Millicent." It was unclear which woman Dr. Phelps was talking about. "She keeps painting the same thing over and over. It's as if she knows no one will see the one she painted last, so she reproduces it again and again." Phelps tsks.

"And no one has found a way to channel her impulses? Train her to paint china or dolls' faces or something in a factory?"

"That's how she landed in here. The supervisors at the factory caught her slipping in little variations here and there. Tiny rhinos in the flower petals on a teacup, a lady's—" she paused, "—nether parts on a dinner plate. Ironic, now that she can paint anything she wants, she continues to do reproductions. Anyway, it's for the best. Her factory job was eliminated a couple years after she came here."

"May I?" I wanted to see if the painting looked anything like I imagined.

"Sure, I'll introduce you. Millicent?" she called ahead seeming not to want to startle her. "Millicent? This is Dr. Bells. He's here to observe us for a while. He'd like to see your painting if that's all right?"

Millicent didn't look up but moved her head a touch. Kept painting.

I expected to see something that looked like a figure of a hostage. Instead, there were strange swaths of color—colors I couldn't remember having ever seen before, brilliant blues, intense yellows, a shade of coral that seemed almost to be laced with lavender and a wild aura of luminescence. I looked for a familiar shape, some sort of line that would show the "hostage." Nothing. Just smears from the woman who could paint the likeness of animals in miniature. This woman was farther gone than I'd imagined.

I looked to Dr. Phelps for some sign of how I should react. The polite second grader in me felt I should say something nice, compliment her for her effort maybe, but the way Dr. Phelps slowly shook her head, eyes closed, I realized an extinguishing response was the preferred treatment protocol. Unbidden, a "*hmm,*" came up in my throat—a *hmm* that said "I can't understand what I'm seeing, but I'm not a complete idiot. I am having *thoughts* about it. I just can't explain them."

Dr. Phelps ignored my reaction and led me toward the door. As it closed behind us, I exhaled a bit too loudly.

"I know. I should have warned you. If you haven't interacted with original artwork for a while—and most people haven't—it can be unsettling."

MY ROOM WAS SMALL BUT COMFORTABLE. A single bed with a coarse bedspread on the left wall, a desk with a reading light on the right. Three drawers were built into a closet next to the washroom.

I unpacked my socks, underwear, and toiletry bag. Had I known Dr. Phelps would recommend wearing standard issue gray—I wouldn't have bothered packing anything else. I agreed with her assumption that dressing like the residents would breed trust. And, honestly, wearing the garb and the new cushiony slipper-socks made my own discomfort dissipate.

By the time I made it back to the common room, Millicent had moved on to a different project, her other painting drying in the corner. I couldn't look at it full-on—didn't want to ruin my relaxed mood by trying to figure it out—but the pop of colors captured my peripheral vision. I couldn't grasp why: maybe the hues' novelty, maybe the light smell of chamomile in the air. Years earlier, Dr. Phelps had delivered a paper on the calming effects of chamomile essential oils on the mood and artistic drive of patients. Post-exposure, their paintings were more pastoral and tranquil than the control groups'.

At the time, I wondered about the ethics of piping in mood-altering oils, but now that I was in the artistic environment, I decided it was just fine. Much preferred to the psychotropics and psychedelics we'd previously prescribe out of hand. Chamomile was much more humane. And ethical. I took a deep, cleansing breath to assert my new position on the aroma.

Two other guests sat at the table with Millicent and the "hostage," who was now gluing miniscule pieces of paper onto bigger pieces of paper that were attached to even larger pieces. If she was going to add another layer, she'd need a magnifying glass. Whereas Millicent had been silent when I'd met her, the hostage—Elizabeth was her name—Elizabeth was all a-chat. "They say you're a doctor. What kind?" She never took her eyes from the work of her hands. "You know what kind of doctor we could use around here? An eye doctor. It's getting harder and harder to see my work. Say…" She looked up at the reading glasses propped on my forehead. "How much for the glasses?"

"How much? Ha!" Millicent chirped one sharp note like a sparrow, then nothing. I wondered if she had received Val-Con when she'd first come here. I estimated her age, considered when Val-Con had been removed from protocols.

"Well, okay," Elizabeth conceded, "I don't have any money, but I could give you a piece of artwork." She *hmphed* dismissively at the piece on the table. "This is paint-by-numbers. I could give you some *real* art." She held my eyes for a second then looked knowingly toward the elevator.

"Liz!" Millicent hissed with alarm, her eyes big.

"Oh, pooh!" Elizabeth brushed her off. "He knows I was just kidding."

I couldn't figure out what I was to think she was kidding about, but I played along.

"Be a doll." Elizabeth pushed a pair of scissors toward me. "Cut this into shapes no bigger than your pinkie nail."

I was about to object then thought of other research questions, new bases for grant applications. The first piece I cut was a triangle. I had intended it to be isosceles, but it turned out to be lopsided. I kept cutting in hopes of evening it out but ended up with a four-sided figure with no parallel sides.

"Spectacular!" Elizabeth declared and snatched the shape from my fingers before I could drop it into the receptacle next to the table.

My participation in Elizabeth's creation failed to draw the attention of the others in the room. For that, I was grateful. A pair of guests continued sketching, and a loner across the room played with a lump of clay on a pottery wheel. I stole glances, not wanting to make them uncomfortable with my gaze. They made what looked like a perfectly good bowl—symmetrical, deep—and then they gave it a karate chop yielding it worthless for holding anything, its side dented in making it look like a grimace. To make it even less usable, they drove their finger straight through the middle of the bottom. They picked it up peeked at me through the hole. Winked.

"Ouch!" I had stuck the top of the scissors under my fingernail. I dropped the scissors on the floor and slid my finger into my mouth.

"Oh, dear." Elizabeth reached out her hand. "Let me look."

I dried my finger on my pants and held it out. The tip was red and throbbing already. The skin was starting to feel taut, and a polyp of blood peeked from under the nail. Elizabeth squeezed the finger next to it as tightly—it seemed—as she could, digging her fingernail in for good measure. I squirmed.

"Sorry about this, honey," she said when she looked into my eyes. "Imagine how good it'll feel when I let go."

And I did. I let myself imagine it. I no longer felt the stabbed finger. It was completely numb. The one she was squeezing hurt so badly it made my eyes water.

"There." She kissed both fingers lightly and gave me back my hand.

Both fingers sang with relief. I wanted to ask her how she had done it, but I was afraid my words would break the spell.

She picked up the scissors, clipped off a corner of the orange paper leaving a whisper of my blood on the rounded shape, and glued it onto her masterpiece.

I couldn't tell when the—collage? paper sculpture? whatever it was—was finished until Elizabeth declared it so. As far as I could see, it was just a weird pile of colored scraps like a topographical map, thick with many layers in some places and only one at sea level.

"Would you like to give it a title?" She said it like she was bestowing a great honor.

A surge of ineptitude washed through me. I was supposed to "get" some meaning out of this mishmash, and all I could think of was a second grade art project. That's what it looked like.

"Oh, you're thinking about it way too seriously." She closed her scissors and put it in a cup on the table. "Whatever it says to your heart, that's the title. There's no wrong answer." She paused, waiting for me to say something I suppose. "I saw your face when you looked at it. What were you thinking?"

"All right, you said there were no wrong answers. I was thinking of second grade and Miss Ellefson."

"Aha! I knew you were remembering something special when you looked at the piece. What was Miss Ellefson's tagline?"

"Tagline?"

"Yeah, the little aphorisms she said to the class. My second-grade teacher always said, 'Where there's a will, there's a way.'" She straightened the leftover paper and slid it onto a shelf behind her. "I had another teacher who always said, 'Anything worth doing is worth doing well.' What did Miss Ellefson always say?"

Until that moment, I had completely forgotten, but Miss Ellefson would hold up her hands in front of her face as if she were discovering them for the first time. "Our hands make us human." Not exactly catchy, but I do remember the intensity with which she said the words. Like she was imparting a great secret. Maybe that was why she'd left so abruptly. I didn't know this at the time, but her departure coincided with the declaration of Artism as a treatable disorder. Now that I thought about it, our classroom walls had been covered with artwork. Framed paintings she'd created by her own hand, interspersed with canvasses we covered with paint. "No construction paper for *us*!"

On the first day of school, she passed out a 11 x 14 canvas to each student, taught us about covering our mistakes with paint, virtually erasing anything we didn't like and getting a fresh go at it with the next layer. What a relief, not having to live with my mistakes. It took the better part of the semester to get my picture to look like I wanted it to, but before we left for winter break, I declared it finished and allowed her to hang it on the wall next to a street scene she had painted when she'd lived in Bangkok.

By the time we returned from break, though, the canvasses were gone. They had been switched out for posters about the parts of speech and messages encouraging us to "Reach for the stars!" and "Make every day count!" Miss Ellefson's replacement, Mr. Hanover, instituted computer coding lessons and something called IBID: Individual Building, Instructional Determination. Everything was done on our "individualized learning platforms," which, at first, we controlled with finger taps but soon exclusively with our eyes. No wonder I'd cut myself when I used the scissors. My hands were woefully out of practice.

"You will need *these* skills to be successful in third grade," Mr. Hanover told us, obviously seeing himself as our savior after an entire semester with a teacher who'd let us paint on canvas and took us on "Noticing Hikes," who'd had us write our observations with invented spellings in pencil on paper, while our technologically superior tablets, which could correct our spelling, sentence structure, and grammar errors, lay abandoned in the classroom.

Miss Ellefson had been such a small blip in my life, I had all but forgotten her, and here I was titling a piece of artwork for her. A piece of artwork, I reminded myself, that would be destroyed as soon as the glue dried.

"*Our Hands.* That's the title," I announced to Elizabeth. "Miss Ellefson said they were what made us human."

"Ah, yes," she clapped her own sinewy ones together. "Now you're speaking my language!" She picked up the piece, 2' x 3', and blew on it gently. Its center dipped slightly, so she put it back on the table. "Tell you what. When it's dry, I want you to have it. You don't even need to give me your glasses. Being able to see clearly would just wreck my impressionist sensibility."

I did want to give her my glasses, but the thought of composing my notes without being able to see clearly—without the ability to delete and replace what I had written—that prospect was too overwhelming. "I need my glasses for the work I must do while I am here, but I'll be happy to leave them with you when I go."

She shot a knowing smile at Millicent. "Well…only if you want to, dear."

THAT NIGHT, I WANTED MORE THAN anything to contact Grey and tell him about my day and the characters I had met. Millicent and Elizabeth, of course, but also Jeremiah, who drew extreme closeups in pencil, closeups so tight you had to stand way back to figure out what they were. It took me the better part of five minutes to figure out the drawing of the lowest thumb knuckle and the fleshy part of the hand, like the scruff of a dog's neck or the loose skin under a turkey's chin. The hand looked to be holding a writing implement, but that was outside the frame of the picture, so I couldn't be sure. As I studied the drawing, I studied my own hand, thinking about what I would write to Grey about my day. Thinking about what he might write back. Though, of course, *that* wasn't going to happen. Grey was long gone, and it was all my fault.

There was a knock on the door. "Dr. Bells?" I didn't recognize the voice. "Dinner is ready. Are you going to join us?"

"Yes, of course." I answered without looking up from my hand. When was the last time I had held a pen or pencil? I used to have them all over the place, in my breast pocket, in my car, in a mug on my desk. "On my way."

Dinner was a family style affair, big platters of food in the middle of the table, a plain white plate in front of each chair. What a nice change from the cafeterias I had grown used to. When was the last time I had offered a basket of warm rolls to the person next to me? Even when I wasn't in a cafeteria, I was being served, as if in a restaurant, by my domestic.

From the conversation, it became clear that the guests each had different levels of contact with the outside world. Some read the "news" on a community com-link though the version of the news made available to them only grazed the change in leadership and the polarization that had taken place as a result. Those who were less informed had the clearer perspective, it seemed to me. Elizabeth was in that camp. "Weren't they belly-aching about polarization with the last leader? How is this one any different?"

Art—yes, an artist named Art (Grey would have gotten a real kick out of that!)—Art chimed in, "Well, I don't know since I have stopped voting all together, but the commentators say she's been bought by the extreme right, that they have funded her for years."

"Right or left?" Elizabeth pushed. "I swear. Yesterday, she was considered a darling of the left."

Art gave a self-satisfied nod. "See what I mean? Polarizing."

As someone who preferred not to think about politics myself, I took this opportunity to observe the mannerisms of those around me.

They weren't markedly different from the people I worked with. Some of the guests chewed with their mouths open. Others took a long, deep breath before making even the smallest, least significant contribution to the conversation. As with any large group, there was one member—in this case Dane—who *hmphed* a lot, shook his head while he cut his meat, and generally acted like he knew what everyone was going to say before they said it, then nodded in self-satisfaction when they did.

On the other hand, there were plenty of differences between these people and those I worked with. In department meetings, I had taken to counting the number of times people made affirmative comments versus contrary ones. As a group, academics were a contrary bunch. But these folks, artists, even when they were disagreeing with each other, left room for the other side to have a reasonable position of their own. Maybe this—and not their creative bent—had been what made them dangerous on the outside.

I dismissed the thought. They had been miserable on the outside, I reminded myself. Here they were happy, in their element. There was no danger of them infecting others, and they could keep producing artwork as their brains had, unfortunately, been hardwired to do.

After dinner, I disappeared into my room to compose my notes for the day. As I worked, my mind kept wandering to Grey and what he might be doing. Answering work communiques, planning a presentation for an upcoming symposium, touching base with his followers to keep them in the loop on his research.

Thinking of him thousands of miles away working at the same time I was, I could almost believe we hadn't broken up. It's not like we'd ever lived in the same space to begin with anyway. Hell, we had never even lived in the same state, but the dailiness of our connections—watching a program and chatting over our com-link, screen-face conversations, masturbating while we talked dirty to each other—and the promise of a stolen weekend in a neutral location had kept the relationship fresh for three good years—and two mediocre ones. I tried not to feel resentful about all the come-ons I had rebuffed—from really interesting, handsome guys—because I was being faithful to Grey. And now. Nothing. Masturbating wasn't the same by yourself.

Without realizing it, I found I was stroking myself under the covers. Instead of Grey's body, I was picturing *Our Hands*, the colors and textures, then other hands: Miss Ellefson's, Elizabeth's, even pompous Art's kneading me and needing me. Their creative impulses pushing into me and me into them. When I orgasmed, it was Millicent's painting that hung before my eyes, the outrageous colors bleeding with the release creating wave after wave after wave. My first orgasm since Grey had ended it.

THE NEXT MORNING, I WAS AWAKENED by the sound of music, a mellow clarinet, trilling violins. The sun seemed exceptionally high in the sky. Perhaps I had turned off my alarm and gone back to sleep without realizing it. I tried to remember the last time I had awoken feeling so well-rested and could not. I opened the shade and looked down onto the lawn where Millicent painted at an easel in the shade.

Another patient—Ram—was dancing, or at least I thought it was dancing. For a time, his body resembled the swaying of a tree in a hurricane. Then it twisted itself into a stiff spire. He balanced on one leg as the other slowly, slowly, slowly lifted straight out to the side, making first a right angle with the ground, then even more slowly making the angle wider and wider until he looked like the 6:00 position on the old-fashioned analog clock at my grandmother's house. My groin ached just watching him. I didn't think the human body could stretch that way.

It was disconcerting to think that everyone else might be up and about while I was still lollygagging in my bed, but, when I got down to breakfast, I noticed I was not the only person with sleep still in my eyes. In fact, three other people were just starting their breakfasts—people I had not seen the day before. They called the meal they were eating "dinner," and, after they finished, yawned and said, "Good night," before clearing their places and, presumably, heading up for a good "night" of sleep.

"The night owls," the one called Opal told me. "We do our best work in the dead of night, so we sleep the day away. At what time is your creative peak?"

"Oh, no." I was about to say, *I'm not one of you,* but caught myself. "I'm just visiting, observing. I don't have a—"

She laughed. "Wait! You're breaking the quarantine? How did you get away with that?"

"I'm here as a scientist. I guess there's no worry of someone like me becoming—"

"Infected!" She laughed again and picked up her bowl and spoon. "You know what's funny? I remember a time when my friends envied my drawing. There used to be classes in school, and the others were jealous when I earned A's. Now those girls—of course they would be women today—would be afraid my impulses would rub off on them."

She poured herself another cup of coffee—and not the decaf either, how would she ever sleep on this bright day with two cups of caffeinated coffee running through her system?—took a sip, and gestured for me to follow her to the common room. "Tell me about your work."

I gave her a brief overview of my research project.

"Do you believe that the suffering from Artism is almost at its end?" she asked.

Suffering. I couldn't tell if she was just playing with me or if she really had felt suffering from her malady. Was she grateful that future generations wouldn't have to feel her pain?

I told her, yes, it looked that way. I didn't want to be specific and tell her that the psychiatric world was waiting for her death and the deaths of the others to declare the disorder eradicated, but she was no dummy. She could extrapolate that from what I had said.

In the corner of the common room sat a cart loaded with Millicent's painting, the potter's useless vessel, and Elizabeth's mound of paper scraps, *Our Hands*.

I wanted desperately to take the art pieces to my room, to keep them forever, but this would be against protocol. Not to mention, it would arouse suspicion.

"I am writing an article about the colony and need some images to accompany the text," I said to the aide sitting at a desk. "May I photograph these pieces before you take them away?"

He looked toward the door as if Dr. Phelps had just walked through it. The only other person in the room besides Opal and myself was Marty, who apparently made sculptures out of found objects. He sat in a corner putting the finishing touches on the form of a man and a windmill—Don Quixote?—out of mini plastic creamer and jelly containers, twist ties and plastic forks. Marty's skin was sallow, the bags under his eyes dark. He hummed one single note to himself over and over. Perhaps there had been some mix-up, a typo maybe, and he belonged in a facility for having Autism instead of Artism? But, of course, those facilities had gone out of fashion long ago.

"Well, okay," said the aide. "But be quick about it."

I snapped a photograph before he could change his mind.

I wondered how he had been inoculated against his daily exposure to artwork. Perhaps there were extensive background checks and DNA testing to make sure he had no genetic predisposition. That was how they'd diagnosed the patients after all. I wondered about this. The coffee creamer guy obviously had no artistic talent, yet he continued to pick up trash and glue it together. I wondered if he had practiced his version of "art" on the outside or if he had picked up this medium once he'd been admitted to try to fit in with the others. Maybe I could get him alone and ask.

With the pictures uploaded and Opal headed up for "bedtime," I headed to join the others outdoors. On the way toward the door, I noticed a cup of pencils and a stack of paper. In the interest of research, I grabbed a handful of each. I had brought along my tablet to work on notes for my chapter and planned to sit on a bench in the shade and act like I was working in order to observe the guests less obtrusively. The second my backside hit the chair, an announcement echoed over the PA. "Yoga will begin in five minutes in the courtyard."

Some people started tidying up. Others kept working. Ram was now bent completely in half, his palms flat on the grass in front of his feet. I was grateful for the bagginess of the gray scrubs we all wore.

"Coming? I brought an extra mat for you." Elizabeth handed me a roll of blue foam. "That cerulean looks great with your dark skin."

I didn't understand what any of the yoga terms meant—or rather what I was supposed to do when the instructor said things like "Downward dog" and "Proud warrior" but soon I picked up the different poses. I started to make mental pictures as she suggested. At first, I couldn't imagine how twisting one leg around the other and doing the same with my arms and reaching for the sky could possibly look anything like an eagle, but, somehow, I let my rational mind go and soon, there was the eagle. I was floating over a canyon, the oranges and reds and tans so vibrant I thought I might cry.

At the end, we lay flat on the ground in a "corpse pose," breathing, breathing, breathing. Soon my breaths became colors flowing into and out of my chest. I must have fallen asleep because when I opened my eyes, the only person still in the courtyard was the instructor who was rolling up her mat.

"You looked so peaceful I didn't want to rouse you." She looped a towel around her neck and held out a hand to help me up. When our hands touched, her face turned serious.

"I thought you were a visitor, but I'm getting the vibe that you might belong here."

I tried to object but knew from her touch that she was right. The test results which had been deemed "inconclusive" when I was a child had been buried because my intellect quotient was so high. My status had been determined when the diagnostic tools were just being developed. The experts of the day believed that one's environment caused 50% of behavior, so they told my parents that feeding my intellect and discouraging creative impulses would be enough.

The older people here in the institution had been too far gone to undergo Extinguishing Therapy. Scientists realized that genes aren't fixed but can be influenced, changed, even mutated throughout one's life with proper surveillance and interventions. Now, babies who showed a predisposition to Artism were put on a strict diet of intellect development and repetitive reward-response activities.

So, yes, as a child, my Artism score had been border-line, and my parents' interventions seemed to have worked because, by the time I graduated from secondary school, there were no discernable markers for Artism, and I was declared art-free. My routine five-year checks had come back clean for the past twenty years, so I knew I would be safe among the art-afflicted. No worries.

Of course, I couldn't let the yoga teacher know any of this. "I get that all the time. I think it's because of the cerulean in my eyes." I let her have a look to show I had nothing to hide.

"You may be right. They really are beautiful."

AFTER DINNER, I DECIDED TO TURN IN EARLY, SO I could wake up at 3 a.m. and see what I could learn from Marty. As I brushed my teeth, I noticed a message from Grey, a few words in the preview window: "I'm sorry. I'm sorry. I'm so—"

My thumb hovered over the button that would reveal the rest of the message. I would never be able to sleep now. I changed into a different pair of scrubs for sleeping and crawled under the covers.

Grey had been the one who had ended things saying I was smothering him with my possessiveness and neediness. How he wanted, just once, to be the one who reached out to me, but I never gave him the chance. Before he could build up any longing for me, there I was anticipating what he was going to ask, telling him things about myself and my day that he hadn't built up any curiosity over.

Well, now it had been three weeks of me not reaching back, resisting the urge more times in a day than I could count. In the past, when I'd had an in-person relationship with someone, I would see them maybe once a day if we lived together. A couple times a week if we didn't. But when there was no hope of in-person connection, there was no need to wait for regular times we would be together. I could contact him while he was in a meeting, his laptop open, naturally, in front of him. One of my favorite things was to send dirty messages to him while he was in his weekly research team meeting.

When we first started seeing each other, that was one of the things he said kept him coming back: my 10:14 missives on first Tuesdays. I loved picturing him at the conference table with a hard-on. A slight flush in his cheeks. I sometimes wondered if that was why things went so well for him at those meetings. All those endorphins streaming through his system. He probably extruded pheromones the others could sense without realizing it. My graduate research suggested they could. Who knows? Maybe they, too, were getting mildly turned on without knowing it. It never occurred to me that I was sending out my own cloud of sex hormones in my monthly department meetings while I sent Grey these naughty messages. Maybe that was why so many of my ideas found fertile ground in those meetings. Maybe that was how I'd convinced the department to support my grant proposal.

I clicked on the button that would show me the rest of his message. Attached was a photograph of our first in-person date. We were at a cabin in the Northwoods, a place completely out of both of our comfort zones. The perfect setting, I knew from research, to stoke attraction. Not exactly "frenetic lust," but our anxiety quotient was just high enough to cement our bond. At least that's what I'd hoped for.

The photo showed us both looking invigorated after a day on the lake struggling to get the canoe to go in a straight line. We were so freshly in love that even the frustration of the shared task—and failure at it—was not enough to make us snap at each other. In fact, our struggles made us more easy-going, laughing at ourselves so as not to show the other what perfectionistic pricks we really were. Or at least that's how I saw it at the time.

Below the photo, Grey's message read like a bad romance novel. *I didn't know what I had until it was gone. I didn't know what we had. Can you ever forgive? How could I ever let you go?* All questions that would have sent me gushing days earlier, but now I wasn't so sure. Maybe because what had passed as passion in our relationship had now become overshadowed by the intensity I was witnessing at the Art Colony, and yes, I was feeling melancholy about the thought of all the devotion that would die with these people—their artwork going into an incinerator. I wondered about the ashes. Would they hold some residual creative spark? Could I make a paste and smear it all over my skin? Could it be absorbed through my pores? I was not as immune as I'd thought I was.

Grey's message would have to wait. I took up the pilfered pencil and started to jot observations from my day. As if guided by an unseen force, my hand swirled out ever more unusual thoughts on the paper. Unusual, but not ridiculous. Not unreasonable. When a particularly elusive idea played at the side of my brain, the pencil would take a break from making words and do a dance that used to be known as doodling. It occurred to me that there was no way to doodle with a keyboard or voice-to-text software. With each curving line of my pencil though, I was able to see fresh connections I hadn't seen before, draw conclusions that just might set the psychiatric world on fire if the right person read them. I filled page after page.

A knock interrupted my scribbles. I shook the cramp out of my hand and slid a blank piece of paper over the notes.

Other than my mealtime reminder the night before, this was the first time anyone had knocked. I opened the door to find Elizabeth in a robe and slippers, her hair pulled back in a headband. "I saw the light under your door. Can't sleep."

The way she said it, I couldn't tell if it was a question for me or a statement about her. I looked at the clock, surprised to see it was past midnight. She entered my room uninvited. I stole a glance at my hand-written notes hoping she wouldn't notice them.

She followed my gaze and picked up the pages, found one with writing, and brought it closer then farther away from her face until she found the sweet spot. Smiled.

I looked over her shoulder to see what she saw. And what she saw surprised me. The first letter of each segment was a hackneyed attempt at an illumination, like in ancient holy texts. The stylized first letters of new sections and chapters were more than building blocks of words but became actual pieces of artwork themselves, with elaborate backgrounds and ornate fonts.

I shrugged. "I didn't—I mean, I don't know—I wasn't aware I was doing it until I heard you knock."

"Well, it's lovely. Bring it down to the community room, and I'll show you where to find the supplies to ink it." She picked up another sheet, and I realized she was holding the notes I had made about her. Thank god she didn't have my reading glasses. They sat on top of my head where I hoped she'd not notice them. I had written a fairly lengthy discussion exploring whether she was "insane" or "gifted," and then came the final sentence: "The two are often in tandem in the individual suffering from Artism." I had yet to make my final judgment about where she landed on the spectrum.

Her eyes lingered on the page. I silently wished I had the stereotypical MD's scratchy handwriting, something we'd joked about in medical school, though I couldn't remember a time any of my own doctors had hand-written a word. In this case though, I had enjoyed the making of letters, the sweep of the pencil, the flourish of the final letter of each word ending as if each one was making its own little promise.

She tidied up the stack of papers and tapped them on the desk to make them line up. "Better yet—"

What was she "better yet-ing?" I needed to focus.

"Let's go downstairs now. We're both awake anyway."

She handed me the papers and headed for the door. I had no choice but to follow. Or at least I felt that way.

In the elevator, I asked whether decorating my notes made them "artwork" in her mind. I couldn't ask aloud my question which was: and if they *were*, would they need to be destroyed? I couldn't bear the thought of Elizabeth learning the true fate of her artwork. She laughed at my question and told me that the market for illuminated manuscripts had long since dried up and I didn't have to worry, as if financial value imbued was necessary for something to be labeled as "art." She knew how to speak the language. "Anyway, it doesn't matter what we call it. I'm sure as a *real* guest—and a researcher—you're not subject to the same restrictions we are. Remember? They'll let you keep it if you want."

We found some bottles of ink and a pen that looked like something out of an old-timey film. "Push this button on the end and the barrel fills with ink." On a piece of scrap paper, she drew a five-petal flower with a smiling face in the middle. The same image I had drawn over and over in the margins of my "Noticing Journal" and that Miss Ellefson had admired so effusively when she'd stopped by my desk to look at my work. The image made me warm inside. A cliche, but also true.

I took the pen in hand and bounced it a couple of times to acclimate to its mass compared to the pencil. I practiced for a time before settling in. I wrote, 'The quick brown fox jumped over the lazy dogs.' Where had that sentence come from? The ink glided onto the paper with a satisfying sweep. Elizabeth found an extra small nib for the tiny outlines on my embellishments, and I used the magnifying glass on a stand to put in the finishing touches.

When I finished, I held up the last sheet and couldn't help myself. "Lovely."

Elizabeth smiled. "Absolutely lovely."

I couldn't leave the pages there to dry, but they would smear if I moved them.

"I know." Elizabeth found containers of paint and small tubs of clay to weigh down the corners. "Here." She handed me a piece of cardboard. "Fan."

She moved her own cardboard just above the papers kicking up enough wind for me to feel it on my face. It felt like summer. I started to fan, too, and noticed the ink drying. The places where it was dry were slightly lighter than the wet spots. Before long, the four sheets were completely dry.

Elizabeth looked pleased. "There, now you can take them back to your room and finish your article or chapter or whatever you're writing."

"A bit of each." I carefully stacked the papers alternating horizontal and vertical just to be sure they didn't smear. "It's silly, though. I'm the only one who will see these." My manuscripts would be sent electronically, of course.

"It's not about who *sees* it, silly," Elizabeth said as if she was talking to a nine-year-old. "It's about who makes it, how it makes *you* feel."

"But—"

"Well, of course, it is important, inspirational, informational for the viewer even, but everyone here will tell you they'll keep making art whether anyone else will ever see it or not." She paused long enough to make me uncomfortable. "We make it even though no one will ever see it."

I was supposed to conclude she was talking hypothetically, but I knew if I met her eyes, they would confirm that she knew exactly what became of all the artwork created in the colony. Nothing.

She took my chin in her hand and tipped my face up, so I had to look at her. "We make it anyway. Maybe that makes us insane." She smiled. "Maybe not."

My skin tingled where she touched. I closed my eyes to break her gaze. There would be no way I would sleep after that. I looked at the clock, faked a yawn. Footsteps echoed in the hall. Like a kid caught stealing candy, I pushed my hands behind my back. Started to think of the story I would tell to explain my presence in the common room and the illuminated sheets of paper. But it was only Marty.

True to form, he made no eye contact. He dropped a plastic bag onto the table and sat in his spot from earlier. He took out a tube of glue and got to work. Tonight, he was working with pen tops and silver gum wrappers. Where had he found this stuff?

Elizabeth greeted him. No response. She asked me, "Ready to call it a day?"

Though I had meant to learn something about Marty and what made him tick, I was pulled to go back to my room to admire my images. I followed her to the elevator.

"If you don't want to be awakened for breakfast, just shift the red button on your door to the left. You can sleep in and grab a snack whenever you decide to get up. That's my plan."

We walked the rest of the way in silence. *We make it anyway.* She hadn't told me in so many words that she knew the pieces would be destroyed, but I was pretty sure she knew. This should have made me feel better: she wouldn't mourn the fact that no one else would ever enjoy her collages. It was about process and not product. She had all but said so. Still, I felt hollow thinking about those ashes.

When I returned to my room, I slid the red button to the left and stared at my creations until the birds began to sing outside my window.

I HAD COME TO THE END OF MY STAY and began to pack my things. I wasn't close to finishing the report I had set out to write, and the case studies and anecdotal evidence I'd hoped to pepper into my report had done more to disprove the theory that Artism was a bonafide mental illness than to confirm it. With the exception of Marty, these people seemed to be wholly sane, well-adjusted, and calm. In fact, I wished more of my colleagues were like them. I wished Grey were more like them. Maybe if he slowed down enough to reflect on his surroundings, tried to make something beautiful in response to them, well, maybe things with us would have worked.

I pulled out my suitcase and dropped in my dirty underwear and socks. I neatly folded my gray scrubs then pictured them being laundered for someone else, told myself they'd never be missed, and tucked them into my bag. Instead of stripping the bed and leaving the sheets in a heap on the floor topped by used towels, I made the bed, neatly refolded the towels and hung them on the bar. Returned the curtains to the position in which I'd found them, half open. Pushed in the desk chair. As if they would wait for me to return.

I clipped my briefcase closed and lifted the handle on my suitcase to roll it across the room. When I opened the door, the sight of Silent Marty, perfectly centered on the mat outside my door, made me jump. I almost didn't recognize him, probably because he looked me straight in the eye. I had never seen his eyes, never noticed the way they caught the light and created the illusion of movement. They were dark, almost black. It was impossible to tell where his irises left off and his pupils began. His hands were tucked behind his back.

I should have greeted him but, for some reason, felt my voice would break whatever spell we were both under.

He showed me his right hand. On it rested the most delicate flower I had ever seen. An orchid? I looked closer to see if it was real, but I couldn't tell. Its pale-yellow petals curled back on themselves, the stamen in the center, an unlikely combination of lavender and dusty green that seemed to continuously change color as his hand trembled. The flower was accompanied by the scent of fresh rain and something faintly mossy. I wanted the thing with a longing that was completely foreign to me.

Afraid to touch it, I asked, "What is it made of?"

"Soap." The first word I had ever heard him speak, a deep baritone that vibrated in my chest. "I make these in my room. The junk art is for show."

Why was he telling me this? He knew that, as a medical doctor, I was obligated to bring something like this to the attention of the director. Residents were strictly forbidden from creating artwork unsupervised. Though, of course, I had done that very thing not so long ago myself. Could he know about that?

"For you." He held the flower closer to me.

I should have said no, thank you. Should have said, I can't accept such things. But words wouldn't come. I put down my bag and opened my briefcase, moved a few things, and grabbed a tissue box from the washroom. I gestured for him to place the flower inside and tufted a few tissues on top to protect it and, to be honest, to hide it. My throat felt like it was in a vice.

"I have a small collection. Would you like to see it?"

We left my things in the room and walked down the hall to his. "Housekeeping doesn't enter my room. I got myself an OCD diagnosis, too, so they have to leave my things alone."

This admission, too, added to the list of things I should report but would not.

The room looked like an art gallery had exploded leaving its entrails strewn about. The walls seemed to be covered with a 3D wallpaper, large and small pieces, each one its own creation and, taken together, something else as well. I slowly took in the art. A paper collage in Elizabeth's style. A miniature of Millicent's hostage painting. Could something here have been created by the hand of Miss Ellefson? A long shot. I started to compose a question I could ask without giving too much away when a piece on the ceiling caught my eye. An elaborate quilt with the line from the nursery rhyme, "The Owl and the Pussycat" stitched in gold thread over an intricately pieced owl and cat.

"May I?"

"Be my guest."

I lay on my back looking up at its magnificence. The owl's head was as big as mine, and the cat's paw reaching toward the viewer seemed to summon me into the image and onto the pea-green boat. At the bottom, the words in script: "And hand in hand, on the edge of the sand, they danced by the light of the moon."

"My most prized possession." He told me about the woman who had made it. She'd been admitted against her will by her wealthy and powerful husband who'd donated a wing to the facility. As he described the husband's background, my shoulders inched toward my ears, my jaw started to clench.

He was telling the story of Matthew Toliver, the unfortunate man who had lost his wife to Artism. Toliver had donated a large part of his considerable wealth to combat the disorder. When the DSM editorial board briefly considered de-listing Artism as a mental illness a decade earlier, Toliver had provided what seemed like unlimited funds to research the disorder. Indeed, some of my graduate work had been supported by the man.

"I loved her, of course." Marty's voice was wistful. "One night when I woke up, the quilt was folded neatly at the foot of my bed. I knew she had—" He worked his jaw a couple times. "That bastard got his wish."

Suicide had long been an issue for people with creative tendencies. In fact, suicide prevention had been one of the first justifications to try to quell creative impulses. I couldn't bear to ask about Miss Ellefson. I comforted myself with the belief that she was decades older than Martin. Their paths could never have crossed. Right?

"From that day on, I have made a point to purchase or barter for a piece of artwork from every artist who has come through the doors." He rubbed his stubbly chin. "I know you're not officially an artist, but I would love to have one of your illuminations."

So he did know.

"I made a place for it right here." He pointed to a spot that looked exactly right for an 8.5" x 11" piece of paper.

My first thought was to demure, tell him I didn't know what he was talking about, but, of course, that would be an insult. I couldn't bear to insult him. Maybe I could tell him I didn't want to part with one, that they were the only drafts of my report, which was due not long after I returned home. Instead, a glimmer of "why not?" floated through my mind, a warmth rose in my chest. I had created something beautiful, and Marty, at some risk, had expressed a wish to have it in his collection. He would see my illumination directly in front of him each morning—or rather each evening—when he woke up. I stopped thinking.

"I'll be right back." Before I could change my mind, I slipped into the hall and hustled back to my room. I found my most beautiful illustration and rolled it into a small tube. I could slip it up inside my sleeve if I came across anyone in the hall.

When I returned, he looked like a child about to receive a gift, expectant and proud. I held it up to him.

He took it and startled me when he wrapped his arms around me. "Thank you," he whispered.

I couldn't find words.

O N THE RETURN FLIGHT, I OPENED my briefcase and shuffled through my remaining pages of notes, being extra careful with those that had illuminations. I dug out an old pad of sticky notes and covered each of my creations in case a nosy seat-neighbor happened to look over my shoulder, though both of them seemed to be deep into watching something inside their VR goggles.

What had I written on the page I'd given to Marty? I took out my tablet and opened the file from which I'd transcribed the notes.

When looking at any form of mental illness, it is informative to observe the behaviors of those suffering in order to ascertain how the disorder affects patients' everyday lives.

Subject: Martin P.

Age: Late sixties (?)

Years at Institution: (Inquire of Dr. Phelps)

Salient Behaviors: The subject makes no eye contact nor speaks even when he is addressed directly. At times, it appears he could be a deaf-mute, but others report having heard him speak though not often. "He just doesn't seem to have anything to say," said one patient. "He speaks through his art," said another.

Patient's artwork consists of gluing together small objects that he has found or taken out of the trash. He seems partial to the disposable items in the cafeteria. Despite the strange medium, Patient's artwork does seem to be representative of a reality. One can recognize the difference between a dog and a horse, for example. He produced a bicycle from jelly containers that was quite realistic though ugly by all objective measures.

Considering his lack of social engagement with those around him and his singularity of focus when he is working on a piece of "art," I conclude he is on the autism spectrum with OCD tendencies. His Artism seems to be a secondary condition and perhaps lends credence to the conclusion that Artism is a condition that has been contrived by the mental health establishment rather than a true disorder.

Blasphemy, in the psychiatric world. I deleted the conclusion.

I hoped that when he read my words, Marty would do so with a sense of irony. I hoped he would get a kick out of the fact that I had "diagnosed" his OCD, the disorder that protected his art collection and his privacy to create masterpieces of his own. I hoped he wouldn't be insulted by the word, ugly, though, as for that, he'd admitted the artwork produced in the common room in the middle of the night was just for show. Undoubtedly, he knew it was being destroyed before the final product was 24 hours old.

But most of all, I hoped he would feel a fondness for my illumination: a W two inches tall and wide with tendrils of sweet pea plants woven through the lines, a tiny imp peeking out from behind the final upsweeping line, the particular blue of the sky in the background, the delicate shading and the pattern of gold curlicues around the border. I hoped that, when he looked at the illumination, he would think of me not as a heartless psychiatrist churning out words for an obscure research project, but as an Artist.

ACKNOWLEDGMENTS

It isn't much good having anything exciting if you can't share it with somebody.

—A. A. Milne, *Winnie-the-Pooh*

Gratefully acknowledged are the following publications, where some of the stories in this collection first appeared or were recognized:

"Jewel Tea," *8142 Review*; 3rd place Hal Prize Fiction Contest

"Numbered Days," *Creative Wisconsin*

"Pay Phone," *A Picture and 1,000 Words*

"Blank," *Moot Point* (as APrayer4You.Com)

"Rink Rat," 2nd place Hal Prize Fiction Contest

I had the great fortune of sharing the journey to this story collection with many people who made it a book of which I am so very proud. Many thanks to those who read portions of the manuscript and helped to make it better: Laura Gordon, Joanne Nelson, Ellice Plant, and Jennifer Rupp. Special thanks to Jane Hamilton and the 10-minute playwriting class members, who planted the seeds for the whole second section of the book. And to my dear friend and beautiful writer, Jane Cawthorne, who took the time and care to read and comment on the whole thing. Jane, you made my sentences crisper and my stories clearer. I am so grateful.

And to the Cornerstone Press staff, especially Eva Nielsen, Chloe Cieszynski, Sophie McPherson, and Ava Willett: thank you for making me part of your college learning and for handling my words with such care and professionalism. Of course, the whole culture of Cornerstone starts at the top with Publisher Dr. Ross Tangedal, who is a champion for writers, for his students, for the press, and for Midwestern literature as a whole. You are such a gift, Ross, thank you. (P.S. – Thanks to your family for sharing you with us, too! No small sacrifice, I know.)

Speaking of family, this book would not exist without mine. Infinite gratitude…

…to my daughter, Shelby, who shows genuine interest in my work, provides a great ear and insights as I muddle through, and always (always!) encourages my reach to exceed my grasp. Plus: long phone chats! I want to be like you when I grow up.

…to my daughter, Ellen, who designed this evocative cover and my author website, who fields my tech questions with patience and provides answers I can understand—and whose own creative pursuits inspire my own. You make my heart full.

…and to Rob, my life partner and best friend, who provides keen insights both on my work and my business, who takes care of lots of the daily stuff so I can spend time with imaginary people and their problems, who supports me without fail. Rob, you make me a better me.

Thank you all so very much.

∞∞∞∞∞∞∞∞∞∞∞∞∞∞∞∞∞∞∞∞∞∞∞

Piglet noticed that even though he had a Very Small Heart, it could hold a rather large amount of Gratitude.

—A. A. Milne, *Winnie-the-Pooh*

KIM SUHR is the award-winning author of *Nothing to Lose* (Cornerstone Press 2018), and her work has appeared in *Midwest Review, 8142 Review, Wisconsin People & Ideas, Moot Point*, and others. She is the director of Red Oak Writing in southeastern Wisconsin.

Printed in the USA
CPSIA information can be obtained
at www.ICGtesting.com
LVHW040424200924
791567LV00008BA/153